THE TRAVEL WRITER

Also by Michael Wilding

Fiction

Aspects of the Dying Process

Living Together

The Short Story Embassy

The West Midland Underground

Scenic Drive

The Phallic Forest

Pacific Highway

Reading the Signs

The Man of Slow Feeling: Selected Short Stories

Under Saturn

Great Climate

Her Most Bizarre Sexual Experience

This is for You

Book of the Reading

Somewhere New: New and Selected Stories

Wildest Dreams

Academia Nuts

Wild Amazement

Superfluous Men

The Plant novels

National Treasure

The Prisoner of Mount Warning

The Magic of It

Asian Dawn

In the Valley of the Weed

Little Demon

Documentary

The Paraguayan Experiment

Raising Spirits, Making Gold & Swapping Wives: The True Adventures of Dr John Dee & Sir Edward Kelly

Wild Bleak Bohemia: Marcus Clarke, Adam Lindsay Gordon and Henry Kendall: A Documentary

Memoir

Wild & Woolley: a Publishing Memoir

Growing Wild

Non-fiction

Milton's Paradise Lost

Cultural Policy in Great Britain (with Michael Green and Richard Hoggart)

Marcus Clarke

Political Fictions

Dragons Teeth: Literature in the English Revolution

Social Visions

The Radical Tradition: Lawson, Furphy, Stead (The Colin Roderick Lectures)

Studies in Classic Australian Fiction

THE TRAVEL WRITER

MICHAEL WILDING

ARCADIA

This is a work of fiction. Names, characters, places and incidents are the products of the author's imagination or are used fictitiously. Any resemblance to actual events, locales, or persons, living or dead, is entirely coincidental.

First published 2018 by ARCADIA
the general books' imprint of

Australian Scholarly Publishing Pty Ltd
7 Lt Lothian St Nth, North Melbourne, Vic 3051
Tel: 03 9329 6963 / Fax: 03 9329 5452
enquiry@scholarly.info / www.scholarly.info

ISBN 978-1-925801-37-8

Cover design Amelia Walker

To Dorothea

Chapter One

The voice on the phone said 'Research. You do research?'

'Yes,' Plant agreed.

'Research assistance. Investigative reporting?' A woman's voice.

'Yes,' Plant agreed. It was what his card said. Business card. Small-business card, maybe that would be better. More accurate, maybe, in these latter days.

'When you say research, what exactly does that mean?'

'Looking things up,' he offered. 'You know,' he said, but he wasn't sure whoever it was did know. 'Like research. Record offices. Data. Libraries.'

Maybe he should have left it at data. Timeless. Contemporary. Libraries sounded historic. Like those words in the dictionary with (obs.) after them. Or (arch.). He was going to have to sit down and cull his vocabulary of obsolete and archaic terms if he wanted to stay in business. Even in small-business.

'Libraries?' the voice said. 'You can do libraries?'

'Yes,' he agreed. Plant the agreeable. He stopped himself from saying 'of course.' He didn't want to give the impression he was someone lost in time in the lost world of books. Even if he was. Or used to be.

'What sort of libraries?'

'Well...' Plant began. He stopped himself from saying anything about books. He could not avoid that anxiety about sounding out of date to a potential client.

'You know,' he said, lamely enough, 'state libraries, university libraries, archives, manuscript collections.'

'Manuscript collections,' the voice said. 'You do manuscript collections?'

'Sure,' Plant agreed.

'And when you say manuscripts,' the voice continued, 'you mean...'

'Well, like manuscripts,' he said. Floundering, no doubt about it. Manu - by hand; script - written. But he stopped himself from spelling it out, just in time. 'You know, collections, correspondence, whatever. Handwritten, typescripts, printouts.'

'Typewritten,' the voice said.

'Yes.'

'Like books that aren't actually books.'

It was one way of putting it. The unborn, the unbaptised, the lost in limbo.

'That sort of thing,' he agreed.

The voice said 'Uh-huh.' The note of excitement or enthusiasm or relief vanished. Just the disembodied words. Neither handwritten nor typewritten nor printed out.

'Can we meet some place?' the voice asked.

'With a view to...?' Plant offered. Tentatively.

'With a view to hiring you.'

'No problem,' Plant agreed.

It was a woman's voice. Beyond that Plant did not speculate. He had been proved wrong so many times, as with so many things. No marked accent. Age indeterminate. Honeyed tones on the phone did not necessarily mean immediate delights in the flesh. Take radio. Or call centres. And the voice on the phone had not sounded especially honeyed. Or anything else. Devoid of resonance, of implication, of suggestion.

So she didn't want to talk about whatever it was on the phone. Sounded promising. He agreed to meet at a cafe in Mullumbimby. Much as he liked Byron Bay he was relieved that she had not suggested meeting there. It was getting too hard to drive into Byron, too much traffic, too hard to find parking. And he preferred to keep his lantana farm private, no reason to let your clients or potential clients know where they could find you. Let alone the people your clients hired you to keep an eye on. Plant believed that the private life of a private eye should be a private matter. Private even as to whether he even had a private life. As far as he could see at the present, he didn't. Same for much of the past. And the foreseeable future too, maybe. But that was his own private business. As for the rest of the past, that was private too and he wouldn't be going back there again in a hurry.

As he crossed the road he looked around to see if he could spot her. She had seen him first and had already stood up. She had been sitting at a table outside on the pavement. No hand outstretched to shake. No touchy-feely embrace. Just a peremptory 'Mr Plant,' no trace of interrogation or doubt. The 'Mr' threw him momentarily. Not how he thought of himself nor how anyone else seemed to think of him. Not usually. But he smiled in acknowledgement, nodded. Beyond words, beyond spoken ones, anyway, as silent as print or manuscripts.

'Thank you for coming,' she said. 'I'm Claire.'

He did the nod and the smile again. He could have said 'no problem' or 'my pleasure' or 'any time.' But he didn't. Not any more.

'My sister,' she said, 'was a writer. You've probably heard of her. Liz Lambastier. The Travel Writer.'

She waited for a response.

'I know the name,' Plant said. 'I'm not sure if I've read anything.'

'She wrote a number of books. Published books,' she added.

Were there any others? Weren't unpublished books manuscripts? Or typescripts? Or computer files?

'She was quite successful. Very, really. And I want to find out if she finished another book before she died that didn't get published.'

Well, she wouldn't have finished it after she died, would she?

'And get hold of it.'

'Ah,' Plant said.

'That's why I was asking about research. I need someone who would know how to find it.'

'I see,' Plant said.

'Can you?'

'Can I what? See?'

'Find it.'

The street life of Mullumbimby passed them by. Third-generation hippies, international tourists, practitioners of the alternative arts and crafts, psychic healers, black magicians.

'It depends where it is, I guess,' he said.

'If I knew that, I wouldn't need you, would I? It might be in her papers, but they haven't been catalogued yet, so there's no way of knowing without working through them.'

'I suppose you wouldn't,' he agreed. 'But there is a collection of her papers, is there?'

'Oh yes. In the State Library. She made sure of that. I thought everyone knew about it.'

'So how big is it?' Plant asked, dodging the issue of why he hadn't known about it. 'How long would it take to work through it?'

'Oh, millennia,' she said.

He blenched. Inwardly. But still a matter of blenching.

'She saved everything. Every little thing. From the beginning. From the moment she decided she was going to be a world figure. From the day that she saw celebrity beckoning. She was absolutely meticulous. Obsessive, really.'

'So this manuscript will be there somewhere.'

'You'd think so.'

'There's no way she would have lost it or anything?'

'No way. Though she might have hidden it somewhere.'

'You think so?'

'What I mean is, if it's not in the papers, that doesn't mean it doesn't exist. She was too caught up in herself ever to lose something like that. I mean, you'd have to look first. But she could have stashed it away somewhere else for some reason.'

'You think?'

'She mightn't have wanted to put all her eggs in the one basket, you know. She was pretty calculating.'

Plant looked at her. She was smiling; bland acceptance of her sister's destiny. But beneath it maybe other feelings lurked. Like a disinclination to work through her sister's papers. Which could result from a number of feelings or motives.

'So what did she keep in her papers?'

'Everything. Poems in the school magazine. Photos of the school choir. School play cast lists. Holiday snaps. Theatre programmes. Invitations. Birthday cards. Love letters. Place cards. You name it.'

'You've seen it, then?'

'No, I just remember her boxing it all up at various times over the years. Or sticking things in scrapbooks.'

'Scrapbooks?'

'Didn't you ever make scrapbooks as a child? Back in the pre-digital age. Big folios of this thick paper, and you'd paste all your postcards and birthday cards and stuff in along with your press cuttings.'

'Press cuttings? As a child?'

'You know, who came first in the egg and spoon race. Cast lists from when she played in some university drama society production. Photographs of her at the zoo. Letters of thanks from famous people she'd foisted her first books onto.'

'And there are a number of these scrapbooks?'

'I imagine so. I don't know how long she kept on making them. All I know is the ones I've ever seen are hideous. The paste shows through the newspaper cuttings like porridge. The paper fades and discolours. The ink smudges. Bits get ripped. She kept them up for years. Like files of diplomatic correspondence from the nineteenth-century. Talk about megalomania.'

'So her papers are not just her manuscripts.'

'Libraries aren't that interested in manuscripts. It's correspondence they like. Gossip. And that's what she assembled. You know, every famous person she'd ever schmoozed up to, she'd keep their letters or business cards or photographs. Carbon copies of letters she wrote to them. How methodical was that, always remembering to insert a carbon and a second sheet? So that way she could be cross-indexed with every minor poet and major celebrity. If you become a footnote in connection with enough people, you develop legs. Soon you're walking high. An important person in your own right. Someone who knew everyone.'

'The woman who knew too many people,' Plant suggested.

'You can't know too many. As long as they're famous.'

'Is that so?'

'That's what she believed.'

'And is it true?'

'They bought her papers, didn't they? So it must have been.'

'She must have been organized to keep it all.'

'She had a press-cuttings agency she subscribed to. So they clipped all the book reviews and interviews and each and every mention of her in the papers.'

'That would have cost.'

'Money was no object when it came to establishing and preserving the myth.'

'Is that so?'

'Pretty obviously. You'll see when you have a look at all the stuff.'

'So you have seen it yourself.'

'I've not actually looked through it. But I saw the boxes when they were collecting it.'

'After she died.'

'No, no. No, she got it all organized while she was still alive. She wasn't going to risk that to posterity. She was going to make sure that it went to a good home if it was the last thing she did.'

'Was it the last thing?'

'No way. As soon as she'd found a library to make a deal with, she got it all organized and packed up. But she could have been working on another book afterwards.'

'What sort of a deal?'

'I don't know. She could have done a straight cash deal. Or it could have been a donation for a tax write-off. Whichever was the best deal at the time, I imagine. I mean, she was into promoting her image but she was into money too. She wouldn't have given it away. Not if she could have sold it or got a tax break.'

'And there's lots.'

'Lots isn't half of it. Heaps. Stacks. Box upon box. They complained.'

'Who did?'

'The people picking it up for the library. They moaned about it. "No one told us there was going to be this much."'

'Really?'

'Yes, really. They had to make two trips. Bring the van back and load up again.'

'But they took it. Two van loads. What size van was it?'

'It was a station wagon. Oh yes, they took it.'

'And now you want me to go through it.'

'That's the idea,' she smiled. Sweetly. But not without a trace of mockery at what she was putting him through. At least that was how Plant read it. But there might have been a note of sympathy there too. He wasn't sure.

'So?' she said.

'So?'

'Can you find it?'

He hated saying 'Well, it all depends.' But he said it.

'Well, it all depends,' he said. 'If it's in her papers, yes.'

Though he didn't want to make it sound too easy in case it wasn't there.

'But what if it isn't?'

'You think it mightn't be?'

'She might have sold it to some other library. She was pretty devious. She had quite a reputation.'

'Uh-huh,' Plant said. 'For what?'

'As a writer.'

As a writer, Plant reflected. And the rest of it, presumably. If she was anything like any of the writers he had encountered. 'So...?'

'So as a writer of some reputation maybe some other library made her an offer.'

'You want me to check out other library holdings. Not just her papers in the State Library. But other manuscript collections. Rare books. That sort of thing.'

'That sort of thing.'

It didn't sound that difficult. If that's all it was. Of course it wouldn't be. Otherwise why hadn't she checked out the catalogues of the obvious libraries? The national, the state libraries, university libraries.

'I don't have time to do it myself.'

She could still check out their holdings online, of course. But why do himself out of a job? So he kept quiet.

'I know I could do an online search, but I need to see it. Make sure it is the book. You can't be sure just from a library catalogue. So it needs someone to do the footwork.'

'That's true,' Plant said.

'And it may not be in a library, it might be with some private collection.'

'Do people collect her work?

'Of course. I'm sure they would.'

'Manuscripts?'

'I don't know.'

'Ah,' Plant said. So libraries, rare-book dealers, private collectors. Left-luggage lockers. Old attics. It could add up to a few weeks work. Or more.

Chapter Two

'So tell me about your sister,' Plant said.

'From the beginning?' she asked and went on before he could reply. 'About our childhood together? Growing up with Liz when we were young?'

Plant gave an involuntary grimace. Or maybe it was voluntary, programmed, triggered by any mention of idyllic childhoods. Or unidyllic. He usually skipped those early chapters of memoir or biography.

'Don't worry. I'm not going to bore you rigid with memories of idyllic times.'

Was he that easy to read?

'Are you that easy to read?' she said. 'Yes, absolutely transparent. You could've been a great mime artist. So calm down. I know what not to say. I'm not going to tell you everything from our very first words. Which were Mama and Dada incidentally. And in that order. Absolutely normative nuclear family. So normative I can't remember anything of any interest about it. Not until we were in our late teens. When life began.'

'Tell me from there,' Plant said.

'Ah, the sex stuff. Is that what you want to hear?'

It wasn't what he wanted to hear at all. Not a catalogue of adolescent affairs. Back-seat gropings. All the unmentionable and all too imaginable.

'Can't help you there, sorry. I was too young and pure and innocent to have anything interesting to tell you about.'

Maybe. He wasn't sure he believed her.

'So tell me about your sister,' he said again. 'Like when did she die?'

'Oh, four years ago. Well, nearer five, now. I thought I'd better start doing something before she's forgotten, otherwise I'd just keep putting it off and it would never get done.'

Plant nodded. How to do something. Put it off for five years and then hire someone else to do it. But it made good sense. No necessity to be cynical. And it got him gainfully employed.

'My sister was a writer. And a traveller. A great traveller.'

'And a great writer?' Plant asked.

'I meant great in the sense that she did a lot of travelling.'

'And did she do a lot of writing?'

'Not as much.'

'How much?'

'She published six books.'

'Travel books?'

'Yes. Travel books. Except for the first which was fiction. Stories. But the others were all travel books.'

'And where did she travel?' Plant asked.

'Oh, everywhere. India. Asia. Turkey. Middle East. Europe. The States. South America.'

'Everywhere,' Plant agreed.

'Pretty much.'

'And she wrote about all these places?'

'Some of them, anyway. She went to so many of them.'

'Doing what?'

'Travelling.'

'Why?'

'To write travel books.'

'Was that why she travelled?'

'She liked travelling. She liked writing. Which came first?'

'You tell me,' Plant said.

'Well, she always wanted to be a writer. From when she was a child. She used to make up these stories.'

'Did she travel as a child?'

'As a child? No. We never went anywhere. I think it was all about escape. Getting away from a boring childhood in the boring suburbs. Making up stories about escaping.'

'And did you escape?'

'I got married,' she said.

'Was that an escape?'

'Have a guess,' she said.

'And your sister. Did she get married?'

'No. Not that I know of.'

'You're not sure?'

'Oddly enough, no.'

'But she might have done?'

'She might have done anything. I don't think she did, but who knows?'

'You weren't close?'

'Not really. We sort of kept in touch over the years but, like I said, she was usually away travelling. So most of the time, no, we weren't that close, as you can imagine.'

He couldn't really. Imagine. He had no idea what either of them was like. Not yet, anyway.

'So why do you need the manuscript if you weren't close?'

'She was family.' She said it as if that explained everything. 'You don't have to be that close if you're family.'

Is that so? he might have said, but didn't.

'To get it published,' she added. 'If it's worth publishing, that is. Assuming she finished it.'

'Why?'

'People are interested in her. In what she wrote.'

'And you?'

'Me?'

'Are you interested?'

'Of course,' she said. She didn't sound so. Not especially. More matter of fact than enthusiastic. If it was a matter of fact.

'And do you think it's likely to be worth publishing?'

'I won't know till I see it, will I?'

'You think there might be some money in it?'

'That would be nice,' she said.

She sounded quite pleased at the idea. Not at all put out by Plant's suggestion. Maybe she didn't think suggestions of making money were demeaning.

'Is anyone interested in it?'

'What do you mean?' she asked.

'Has anyone approached you?'

She looked blank.

'A publisher or...'

'Oh, I see what you mean. No. Not in so many words. But I thought if someone was sort of interested in reprinting one of her books and if it did well, you know...'

'They might want more.'

'That's right,' she said.

'But no firm offers.'

She shook her head. 'No.'

Which all sounded convincing enough.

'I want to get her work organized before...'

She faded away.

'Before it fades,' she began again, reaching out for the word before it dissolved and disappeared.

'Organized?' Plant said.

'You know, back in print, a collected edition.'

'Those were the days,' he said.

Rows of uniform bindings, gilt lettering, major works, minor works, collected essays and reviews.

'What were?'

'The days of the collected edition.'

'Don't they have them any more?'

'I don't know.'

'And e-books,' she said. 'I want to make it all available electronically, too.'

'Before it fades.'

'Before the interest fades. It's a matter of letting people know the work is out there.'

'And that's why you're looking for anything unpublished.'

'Well, yes,' she said.

'Even if there isn't anything.'

'How would one know without looking?' she asked.

'Have you got a publisher in mind?'

'Not really.'

'I'd start with someone who's already published her.'

'I suppose so,' she said. 'Unless they'd vowed never to touch her books again.'

'Is that likely?'

'She could annoy people.'

'And she annoyed her publishers?'

'Why not? She annoyed everyone else. Big time.'

'You might have your work cut out.'

'It will be something to do. Fill up the empty hours.'

'Are they that empty?

'Aren't yours?' she asked.

Were they? His hours? So empty? Dare he admit it? Would it matter?

'I keep busy,' he said.

'Papering over the emptiness.'

She could have been right.

'What about Liz?' he asked. 'Was that why she wrote and travelled? To paper over the emptiness?'

'Probably,' she said. 'Except that she'd never have let on. She always kept busy. She always seemed to believe in something she had to do.'

'Seemed to?'

'Well,' she pondered. 'You've got to wonder, or I wonder, when you believe in so many things, like Liz did, whether you really believe in any of them. I mean she was always into this or that and then she'd move on to something else and on she'd go. And I'd just be sitting there like Little Miss Muffet trying to think of something to do. So I don't know.'

'And you never got caught up in any of these enthusiasms?'

'Oh, I got caught up in them. All of them when we were young. She'd drag me along to these poetry readings and art galleries and protest meetings and stuff, and I'd get all caught up in it, whatever it was, and by the time I'd surfaced she'd've moved on. You know. "No, too boring darling, done that, been there, no future in that."'

'Like what?'

'Like poetry to begin with.'

'Poetry?'

'She always wanted to write. She wanted to be up there, out there.'

'Not your average hide behind the keyboard writer, then.'

'What do you mean?'

'A lot of writers write because they don't like public appearances. They prefer to hide in the shadows and throw their words into the arena like paper darts.'

'Paper darts?' she said. 'Wow, how's that for a trip down memory lane?'

'Didn't you ever throw them?'

'Of course, but I doubt that anyone knows what they are any more.'

She could have been right. Day by day the world spun on and changed irrevocably.

'Anyway, she wanted to write, you say.'

'You've confused me now,' she said. 'Maybe it wasn't so much about the writing, maybe it was more about the performing. Being seen. Holding an audience.'

Plant nodded.

'I mean, she used to write these poems. But what she really liked was reciting them now I come to think about it.'

'The two aren't necessarily incompatible,' Plant offered, generously.

'No,' she agreed. 'Perhaps not. She'd drag me along to these dreadful galleries in East Sydney and Paddington. Not that I thought they were dreadful then. Back then they were the height of sophistication and excitement to me. Can you imagine? The naivety of it.' She laughed. 'But it's all part of life, isn't it? It still goes on. All those earnest temple gatherings to money and exclusiveness under the guise of art. Ah well. We all fell for it. Flowing fabrics and fancy dress and the tedium of it all, walls covered with abstraction and all those poets standing up and performing, one after another.'

'And how did she like it?'

'She loved it. To begin with, anyway. She could look good. She could make herself attractive. And she was young, of course. So she attracted attention. Naturally.'

'And you?'

'Oh, I just hid in a corner and merged with the shadows.'

He wasn't sure that he believed her. Once again.

'In the end she saw that it wasn't her scene. The writers didn't belong there. It was all about money. Rich people with the means to buy expensive paintings. Writers didn't figure, they hadn't worked out how to suck up to the rich and get them to pay through the nose for a poem. They tried poster poems, hang them on your walls, but they didn't really work. Artists need rich patrons. That's why they hang out in the socialite scene. But writers need publishers. So she figured out galleries and poetry readings were pretty much a waste of time. Or eventually she figured it out. Thank heavens. Once you've seen one tired old junky poseur propping up the door frame in his look-at-me artistic clothes and artist's hairdo you've seen the lot. To say nothing of the tired old derivative daubs on the walls. All totally obscure, empty posturing. But that was the point, to distinguish the connoisseurs from the rest of us. The cognoscenti. Aesthetic souls. Whatever they called themselves.'

She gave a laugh of dismissal. An amused laugh, amused at the idiocy of the world but not embittered.

'I think Liz realized pretty quickly that while it might seem hip and cool and whatever the current word of approval was to be avant-garde and artistic and alternative and to publish poems in obscure magazines with two hundred maximum circulation, more people actually read the mainstream magazines. Including your hip, cool fellow poets. And the mainstream magazines paid. If you gave up poetry and turned to prose. So there seemed no virtue in hanging out with the artistic alternative. And no sense either. She was smart. She soon realized the name of the game. Of the game she wanted, anyway. One of the first to jump ship. Out of Bohemia and into the big time.

'These were the good times. People like Liz enjoyed themselves. There was hope. They felt they could do things, make things, write things, achieve things, make a difference. Maybe the causes were false, maybe people sold out, almost certainly they did, but they were good times while they lasted. Which I'm not sure they are now.'

So Lambastier left the world of the art galleries and their socialite patrons. She was not alone in that. Some of the poets mutated into novelists, much to the earlier novelists' resentment. Some of the novelists turned to the market and wrote novels of sex and romance and crime. But Lambastier abandoned poetry, abandoned short stories, bypassed novels, and made her way into journalism, travelling to fabled and exotic places and interviewing rich and famous celebrities until she had transformed herself into a rich and famous and fabled and exotic celebrity herself.

'So,' she said. 'Are you interested?'

'I could be,' he said.

'But?'

'But I'll need to spend some time in Sydney. Canberra, maybe. Checking out libraries.'

'Is that a problem?

'Not for me especially. But it bumps up the expenses. Accommodation and so on.'

'You can stay at my place in Sydney,' she said. 'I'm up here at the moment, so it's not occupied. You'll have the place to yourself. Anyway, there's lots of room, even if I was there.' Which she wasn't going to be.

Plant considered it.

It would save him from having to look for somewhere. And save her from having to pay his hotel bills. He hadn't been planning to stay in a hotel, though now that he thought about it, it had its appeals. Certainly preferable to staying with Fullalove in his unrenovated, ungentrified, inner-city hovel, more like a book depository than human accommodation.

'It's in Neutral Bay,' she said. 'It's not some inner-city dive crawling with cockroaches. You can use the guest room. Clean sheets on the bed.'

'How will I know which is the guest room?'

'You'll work it out, I'm sure. Use your investigative skills.'

'A house or an apartment?'

'An apartment,' she said. 'You won't have to keep the lawns mown. But there's off-street parking.'

'Brilliant.'

'That's settled then.'

'Are you sure it's all right?' he asked.

'I wouldn't have suggested it if it wasn't, would I?' she said.

He didn't know.

'I suppose not,' he said.

'You suppose correctly,' she said.

She gave him the keys and the security code.

'You're sure you're happy with this?' he asked.

'It should save me a couple of hundred dollars a day expenses, shouldn't it?' she said. 'That makes me happy.'

Afterwards he found it hard to describe her. Couldn't remember what she looked like. Conventional. Ordinary. Distinctly unremarkable. It said a lot for his powers of observation and his skills as an investigator. Well, I am a researcher, not a camera, he told himself. Maybe he was developing that medical condition which left you unable to memorize faces. A lot to be said for it. Or maybe she had developed a strategy that thwarted recognition devices, digital, photographic, human. Whatever, however, she was gone, vanished. Leaving him the address and the key in his pocket.

Chapter Three

The apartment was high up in a high-rise on a high point of Neutral Bay, floor fifteen, with a panoramic view of the lower north shore and across to the harbour and the city. The harbour that was always there for the city, even if sometimes just in water glimpses, stand in the corner of the kitchen on a chair and you'll see it, the real estate agent pitch, always a chance to see a sliver of the harbour or Middle Harbour or the ocean.

Plant loved his rural retreat, his lantana farm hideaway, trees and more trees and the fragment of a creek, snakes and goannas, wallabies, and a celestial aviary of bird life. More and more he was settling into rustication. He had never been that keen on the idea of apartments. He felt safer with his feet close to the ground. But he could see the attractions. Airy. Almost an eyrie. Free of the feelings of constriction that terraces always gave him.

And if you had to live in a city, then live in a city with views of the water, with the ceaseless traffic of the harbour, the arrivals and departures, not just ferries but ocean liners, even if these days they were all cruise ships, no longer the lifeline to other continents. But they brought in the vision of escape, of travel, of other realms, realms you didn't even have to travel to, just be reminded of the possibilities, the illusion of the limitless. Was that what had inspired Liz Lambastier, the early sight of those ships, the assertion of other lands to visit, to explore, to record, to conquer, to relate? You could fix on aircraft, too, but somehow they did not evoke the same responses, just memories of cramped seats and threats of deep vein thrombosis. Anyway, it wasn't just the travel, it was the lure of emptiness, the excitement of the uncovered, the unbuilt-on, the untameable, that ocean of the mind, that harbour of the unconscious, unbidden thoughts nestling there, the unexplored potential, a sense of the infinite in the finite.

It was a sizeable apartment. He found the guest room, spare and bare, which suited him. Back in the living room the walls were lined with bookshelves. And the shelves were full of books, not china or wood carvings or family photographs. It was furnished simply, uncluttered. No obvious impress of Claire's personality. Amazingly free from it, indeed. Which suited Plant. He had no wish to burrow into some other creature's presence, like a tick or a tapeworm. There was a smart television, a CD player and radio, a neat case of CDs, a table, couch, chairs, but it was the books that gave the place its feel. A slightly old-fashioned feel to it with the books and the compact discs. That and the panoramic views. He alternated between looking at bays of books and windows on the world. The books gave a sense of some sort of comfort, some traditional values, some settled way of life. He didn't know why. Maybe because he so rarely saw shelves of books in the places he visited. Somehow to see them here was reassuring. Plant was comfortable with that. More than comfortable: at ease. He checked out the way the books were shelved. Some people arranged them by subject, some by size, some by colour. These were arranged by author in alphabetical order. One system taking in all the shelves. The only way in Plant's opinion. It suggested a working library. Not primarily decorative or the spoils of a collector. He wondered what she used it for, was she a teacher or a mature student or another writer like her sister? He realized she had not told him anything about herself. Rare in his experience. Admirable and welcome, indeed. Except he should have asked a few things. He was getting too self-protective, too eager to avoid the tedious, too grateful for being spared the boring. He was starting to miss things.

Registering that, he took himself to the approximate middle of the shelving. Where the authors beginning with the letter L were shelved. He looked for Liz Lambastier. And she wasn't there. Not a book. Not a pamphlet. Not a cutting. Not an offprint. Family values, he speculated. Sibling rivalry. Unless of course there was a complete collection which she carried around with her, took up the coast when she was staying up there. Which seemed unlikely. There was no separate display cabinet anywhere else in the room that might have housed them. There was no sign of Lambastier's books anywhere. The mystery of the missing books. Something else to puzzle over while he searched for the missing manuscript. He nosed round the kitchen and switched on the electric jug and found a teabag and made himself a cup of tea.

He sat back in one of the armchairs and enjoyed it all, civilization, comfort. Even the armchair was comfortable, which was a rare bonus. All very cosy. Or at least cosy enough. Tomorrow he'd buy some milk, in the meantime black tea.

He let his eyes wander around the room, across the windows, the bookshelves, the ceiling. He was not consciously looking for surveillance devices but he spotted one nonetheless, imitating a sprinkler system or a smoke alarm, some little technological pustule protruding from the ceiling. A camera. No doubt there was surveillance everywhere. Otherwise she wouldn't have let him into her apartment so readily, would she? It had seemed unusually convenient and generous. Was it her way of keeping an eye on him? Not inconceivable. No way he was going to be able to smoke anything here. And not just because there weren't any ashtrays scattered around. No need for 'No Smoking' signs. Though there was one on the door of the fridge. Nor could he even go down to the car and roll up a joint and drive off and have a smoke, that was just inviting trouble with all the testing equipment they told you that every police car was carrying. Couldn't risk it driving, couldn't risk it parked at the side of the road or in a car park. Or in a public park. Or on the beach. Welcome to surveillance city.

But he could call in on Fullalove, seek out sanctuary there, like a medieval church.

Chapter Four

Plant had to check in with Fullalove, anyway. Even if he wasn't staying with him. Thank heavens. But basic courtesy, even with Fullalove, demanded that he visit. Like reconnecting with your imaginary friend. And Fullalove's take on things was always useful, even if it was getting increasingly difficult to enter his house. Fullalove's project to stockpile copies of any book likely to provoke disapproval from the guardians of political correctness, and to market them to people who wanted their reading to leave no digital trace, had expanded beyond Plant's wildest nightmares. It had developed beyond mere obsession. The hallway of his inner-city hovel was lined both sides, floor to ceiling, with bookshelves packed solid with books, leaving only the narrowest corridor to squeeze through. Every room was lined with shelves, all filled with books, all lined upright, with the space between them and the shelf above crammed tight with books lying horizontally. Books totally surrounded every room, covered every wall to the ceiling, shelf upon shelf, and sat in stacks in front of the bookshelves. Books were piled on the kitchen table. You had to eat between them and the newspapers encroaching on every side. Unless you moved to one of the old maroon velveteen armchairs, and the books were stacked each side of them, leaning against the chair sides for support. Plant felt he might become like the portrait of the Emperor Rudolf II, the one composed of books.

'You'd rather be like the one composed of vegetables?' Fullalove asked, showing an unsuspected familiarity with Renaissance art.

Plant wasn't sure he wanted to be like either of them.

'Great insulation,' Fullalove said. 'Cuts down on heating bills now they've privatized electricity and the cost has rocketed up. Keeps it cool in summer.'

Not that it seemed cool to Plant. Stifling and oppressive, in fact. Fullalove's insistence that they went out before they talked was, for all its irritating paranoid obsessiveness, a great relief. Though first of all there was the business of rolling up a number. And smoking it. No way Fullalove was going out into the world unprepared, unfortified. Nor Plant.

And Fullalove was not only sympathetic, but had a solution to Plant's woes.

'Cook it.'

'Cook it?'

'No need to smoke it, it'll set off the smoke alarms and she'll see you rolling it. Get yourself some foil, here.'

He produced a roll of supermarket home-brand cooking foil from a kitchen drawer and ripped off a strip and then ripped the strip into small rectangles.

'Give me your dope,' he instructed.

Plant handed it over, and Fullalove shredded a small pile onto each rectangle, the equivalent of a good-sized jumbo joint on each one. Then he folded the foil tightly round the dope.

'Boil it in a saucepan for about fifteen or twenty minutes. Activates the THC. If they see you on camera they'll think you're boiling Chinese herbs or something. You'll find it lasts longer than smoking it. Better for your lungs and heart. And more economical, too. Boil up one a day, or two if pain persists. Doctor's orders. Medicinal marijuana, mate, if anyone asks.'

'You're a genius,' Plant said, overcome with relief. The world glowed with hope and goodwill again.

'All part of the service,' Fullalove said, taking a couple of substantial-looking heads from Plant's stash as a service fee.

Outside in the street there were signs of the beginnings of a southerly change. Eddies of air stirring up litter and leaves amidst the exhaust emissions and air-conditioning exudations.

'You're going to have to rent a storage facility,' Plant said.

'I already have.'

'Have you actually sold any books yet?'

'I'm working on it.'

'Working on it?'

'Fine-tuning.'

'It's insane.'

'No it's not. It's fascinating. Quite cheering, in fact. To see how much of our cultural tradition is now deemed unacceptable. It makes you realize what a privileged world we grew up in. I hadn't realized that until I looked into it.'

'But now you have.'

'Now I have and I intend to keep it that way.'

'What way precisely?'

'Free and open and exciting and adventurous and stimulating and fun. Fun,' he repeated. 'It's made me realize that there's no point going on about how dreadful the world is. Of course it is. It always has been. Just be grateful you lived when you did.'

'I'm still living,' Plant pointed out.

'No, but really living. In the days when the world was wide. Sex, drugs, books. We had the good times. The best times. Just think how lucky we were and appreciate it.'

'The trouble with those years is we'll never know who was authentic and who wasn't,' Plant reflected.

'There were always frauds and opportunists and informers and provocateurs in any era. The Gunpowder Plot, for instance...'

'It makes you wary of any commitment.'

'That's the point.'

'I don't think people looked obviously inauthentic in order to make everyone else doubt the possibility of any authenticity.'

'Why not? Perfect model of social control. And if plan A fails, move to plan B. If people are revealed to be frauds, that creates doubts. If they're not exposed, they just lead people astray. Either way the system wins.'

'You really believe it's all as manipulated as that?' Plant asked

'Of course. Take political correctness. A perfect way to create reaction. Women's movement, gay and lesbian rights, identity politics, this all gets presented as the culmination of the good times of 60s and 70s radicalism, it serves to displace the real leftist issues of class and economic injustice and so in effect it destroys the left. And it ends up as such an excessive, oppressive illiberal movement that it finally provokes the desired result – extreme reactionary politics. Which we've got now. Neat, if you like that sort of thing.'

'Do you have to see it all as a conspiracy?'

'Pretty much. Take global warming. Forget all the alarmist stuff about the hottest day since whenever. So what? Why wouldn't it be? Nature's variety. The climate has always changed, it's always either getting hotter or colder. There's no static state in nature, static state means death. If they really believed global warming was man-made and they were really serious about it, they'd say, use less power. Prohibit lights left on all night in office tower blocks. Stop illuminating the Harbour Bridge. Cancel the New Year fireworks.

'Forget all the stuff about the evils of coal-fired power stations. Forget alternative renewable sources. What they really want to do is create a climate of fear about allegedly man-made climate change so that they can introduce large scale atomic energy reactors. And that way produce the by-products for nuclear weapons. It's all about atomic energy. And atomic energy's all about military aggression.'

'Have you ever considered that your disillusion and cynicism are convenient excuses for non-involvement?' Plant said.

'Who needs an excuse?'

'You avoid committing yourself by saying all politicians are the same, they offer no alternative choices, and they're all corrupt.'

'Pretty much,' Fullalove agreed.

'So why were the 60s and 70s such good times?'

'We were young then.'

'People are young now. But if you were alive and young now you'd be hard put to find any good times.'

'I am alive now,' Fullalove said.

'But not young. Look at you. It's all over.'

Fullalove gave his quizzical look.

'I look back on the good times with gratitude,' he said. 'And I'm going to keep those good times alive.'

'By selling dirty books at excessive prices to people who don't want to be found out reading them online or purchasing them by credit card or borrowing them from a library.'

'What's excessive?'

Plant ventured no reply.

'It's a matter of what the market will bear. The free market. Cornerstone of the way we live now.'

'You don't like the way we live now. You've always opposed a market economy.'

'Hate it. But might as well make a buck or two out of it before it implodes.'

'By peddling filth.'

'Not necessarily. It's all in the eye of the beholder. One woman's filth might be another chap's sustaining vision. You've got to stop being censorious.'

'Me?' Plant said. Outraged.

'Calling stuff filth. Anything that is sexually, politically or economically liberating, they're trying to suppress by labelling it sexist or unacceptable or inappropriate or some other weaselly word. It's a purge.'

'And you're saving the day. Preserving the cultural heritage from the barbarians within the gates.'

'Couldn't have put it better myself.'

'Providing anything that people don't want recorded on their bookshop purchases or library borrowings or e-book downloads.'

'Exactly.'

'Cash only.'

'Obviously.'

'Glad it makes you happy.'

'Thank you. It certainly does.'

And that was something, Fullalove not someone habitually prone to happiness, his millenarian world view conceding a future hope, but not much joy in the immediate situation.

They walked along King Street, past the Thai restaurants and Indian diners and clothing outlets and more Thai restaurants and Indian diners and Mexican restaurants and clothing outlets. Fullalove ducked into the narrow dark frontage of a narrow dark cafe. It was empty, unpatronised, which normally Plant would have taken as the sign of a place no one wanted to go to, bad coffee, bad food, bad vibes. But its emptiness was welcome after the jostling, blundering pedestrians on the pavements and the grinding, groaning, rumbling of the trucks and buses and cars starting and stopping and idling and accelerating and braking on the road. And its emptiness appealed to Fullalove, something that reduced surveillance opportunities; with no one else there, there was less chance of conversations being overheard.

'Do you have any of Lambastier's books in your hoard? Do you know what you've got there?'

'Oddly enough, yes, I do know what I have, more or less, and no, I don't have any of her books.'

'Not enough filth and porn and political incorrectness for you?'

'Up to a point.'

'Up to a point?'

'There's a sort of sexy suggestiveness she works at when she wants to. And then she goes all squeaky clean and PC. And all the liberal bullshit. I stack her away with the enemy.'

'The enemy?'

'Boxes of evidence of the soft fascism we live under now.'

'Waiting for the next Nuremberg trials.'

'No, can't be bothered. Just shit I bought in job lots or by mistake. I bundle it up and sell it on. Take it to the charity shops. Get rid of it as soon as possible.'

'You don't want stuff like that contaminating your stock,' Plant suggested. Somewhat sceptically. But Fullalove agreed.

'Too right. Bloody lethal.'

'Like radioactivity?' Plant asked.

'Pretty much,' Fullalove agreed. 'I can look out for her if you want.'

'No worries. It's this unpublished manuscript I've got to track down.'

'What's it about?'

'No idea.'

'So you don't know whether it's a bodice-ripper novel or a kiss-and-tell misery memoir.'

'Not sure that it's either.'

'It would need to be more than that to get any interest in today's market. Got to be a transgender asylum seeker turned suicide jihadist hacker at the very least. Won't get a look in for anything less.'

'The impression I've got is she was always able to adjust to market forces.'

'But she's dead, isn't she? She won't be doing any adjusting now.'

'That's true.'

'Someone ghosting the manuscript, is that it? You're up to your old tricks again.'

Plant had done some ghost writing. Like he'd done some journalism and some delivery work and some farm work. Casual. Like work in general these days. None of it anything he wanted to be remembered for or identified with.

'Not me,' he said. 'But it could be someone could fake it, I suppose. I hadn't thought of that.'

'Someone slips a pristine hot copy into the rare books collection just before our intrepid explorer stumbles across it and rescues it for the world.'

'Not impossible.'

'How would you ever know? Carbon date the paper? They'd have thought of that for sure. Get some old paper stock. Or print it out on the back of an old typescript. Easy.'

'A lot of trouble to go to,' Plant said. Always keen to minimize trouble.

'Nothing compared to faking old masters. Aboriginal art was easy enough. A lot of folk got into faking that. No problem. But old masters, that takes a lot of skill. Or old mistresses. Mistresses might be the trick. More scope there. Discover the suppressed, hidden, forgotten, imprisoned but now newly discovered old mistresses. Surprised no one's done it. Maybe they have. I mean think about it, books, forget books compared with fine art. That's where the money is. Dirty money. And the paintings are like collateral. Another currency. Pity you can't put the same value on manuscripts. Maybe you could. It's worth looking into.'

Fullalove wiped the flecks of cappuccino from his face. His eyes gave some intermittent sparkles. Another project.

'You're going to start faking paintings now?'

'Not necessarily.'

'Manuscripts, then? You're not going to start speculating in manuscripts? Or faking them, is that it now?'

'Just a thought,' Fullalove said, smiling to himself, which Plant took as a sure sign he was thinking about it and enjoying the thought. 'Especially if the material had a financial potential. Like blackmail. Have you thought of that?'

'No,' said Plant. He hadn't thought of that.

'Well, think about it. Is that what your musty old missing manuscript mystery is about? She spills the beans on a few old bean-counters she's fucked along the way. Someone's keen to get the dirt to do a bit of blackmail. Or alternatively someone wants to stop the dirt ever getting out and the blackmail ever starting. So a pre-emptive strike. Can't see why anyone else would be interested.'

'You always go for the seedy side of things.'

'Sure do,' Fullalove agreed.

'There's no suggestion that blackmail's an issue.'

'There wouldn't be.'

'It's a matter of getting an unpublished book published. Literature, you know? There's interest in her work.'

‘Is that so?’

‘Obviously. That’s why her sister’s hired me.’

‘And you believe that?’ Fullalove asked.

Plant looked across. Fullalove looked back, cappuccino foam flecked, unshaven, unkempt. And that irritating expression of quizzical disdain. No doubt Plant’s own expression was one of no less irritatingly familiar irritation. He could feel his stomach wrenching and struggling with the coffee.

‘Probably not,’ he agreed.

Chapter Five

Claire hadn't brought any of her sister's books along to give to Plant. She hadn't thought it necessary. It was the unpublished one she needed. Needed rather than wanted, that was how she put it. He filed it away for later consideration. As for the books, she conceded that reading them, one or two of them, might give him some picture of her sister if he felt he needed one. Though it was clear she didn't think he did. Need a picture. She hadn't even brought a photograph. 'Charge them to expenses, why don't you, if you feel you have to have them,' she said. A second search of the apartment's bookshelves still didn't deliver any of Lambastier's books.

Which was why he called in at Mac Arber's rare and collectable books in Glebe. The shop proclaimed Arber in elegant gold lettering, with a couple of green trees each side of the name. He could have searched online, they books would be available somewhere and Mac might not have copies in stock, but why let the world, or certain components of the world, know what you were looking for? And it was worth dropping in on Mac, usually. A mine of information. Gossip central. Studies in Contemporary Literary History. Not necessarily any more secure than the internet, of course. But with a human face.

He opened the door and the irritating little bell rang, an insincere evocation of some cosy past age of taste and culture and book collecting. Plant found it so anyway, irritating and insincere, but he acknowledged that he could be wrong.

'You are a very lucky man,' Mac Arber said, when Plant asked for Lambastier.

The smell of burning incense hung heavily over the room. Or burning something. It was like having your horoscope read in a fortune-teller's tent. The huge hopes, the great promises. And rarely that much to show for it.

Unless a copy of just one of Liz Lambastier's books standing there on the shelves was the embodiment of luck. Plant was not fully convinced. But one of her books was better than none. Its instant accessibility could be interpreted as a positive sign. If Plant had been the sort of person who looked for signs of hope. He used to. In the past. Now he rarely bothered. The effort of being hopeful generally outweighed the meagre results. But he did his best to smile all the same.

'Is that it?' he asked, bringing it to the counter.

'That's it.'

'No others?'

'What you see is what you get. As long as you pay for it.'

Plant wasn't sure about that. Were all Mac's treasured wares on display? Somehow he doubted it. But he was sure Mac knew what stock he had.

'How about manuscripts?' he asked.

'Oh, manuscripts,' Mac said. 'Very tricky. Very specialized. You can end up with an awful lot of waste paper if you're not careful.'

'And you're careful.'

'Naturally. It's a specialist trade. Not a lot of demand, as you might expect.'

'What about her?'

'What about her? You mean are there manuscripts of hers floating around? Why? Are you in hot pursuit?'

'Just wondered,' Plant said.

'No you didn't. You have something specific in mind, I know you. Be honest.'

'I'm always honest.'

'I doubt that. It would be admirable but foolhardy. Come clean, Plant, let me know and I might be able to help you.'

He said it in tones of such insinuating care that Plant felt positively threatened.

‘I just wondered if there was any stuff of hers still unpublished.’

‘I should imagine so,’ Mac said. ‘Most of these writers have boxes of stuff, as you so elegantly put it, that no one would ever want to publish. Especially these days. They go out of fashion. Demand falls away. Who cares any more?’

‘Does nobody?’

‘Presumably somebody does or you wouldn’t be asking. Come clean, Plant.’

‘There’s supposed to be some last manuscript she never published.’

‘And?’

‘And her sister wants it.’

‘Her sister.’

‘Yes.’

‘Is this family sentiment or low finance?’

‘Nobody’s offering big money for it as far as I know, if that’s what you mean.’

‘That’s what I mean.’

‘Can’t answer.’

‘Can’t or won’t.’

‘Can’t. I don’t know. I don’t know if anyone would want it or if it’s any good or if it even exists.’

‘I suppose you could always fake it,’ Mac offered.

‘If I knew what it was supposed to be about.’

‘And you don’t?’

‘No.’

‘Fact or fiction?’

‘Dunno.’

‘That leaves a wide field.’

‘Yes,’ Plant agreed.

‘A little fire in a wide field is like an old lecher’s heart.’

‘Is that so?’

‘According to the Bard.’

Mac fiddled around at his computer, summoning up what there was on Liz Lambastier's oeuvre.

'Wasn't she one of those writers who wrote a book about being on the game? Or was it about having a terrible mother or an absent father? Or maybe a deranged husband or cloyingly loving stepchildren?'

'I don't know,' Plant said. 'I haven't read her yet.'

'You could never tell with those girls. Such a tease. She might have made it all up. How would I know, after all? There was a whole, what should I say, a whole brothel of them. It became quite the fashionable literary theme. *Between Careers*, *The Happy Hooker*, *The Hite Report*. Internationally, too. I mean, it wasn't just here. Well, nothing ever is, is it?'

'Were they fact or fiction?'

'Who can tell? A bit of both, I would imagine. I have them all in stock. Maybe you should buy them for some sort of context.'

'Maybe,' Plant said. 'How do you know she was on the game? Don't tell me from personal experience.'

'Really,' Mac said.

'So how do you know?'

'It was the talk of the town back in those days. Ultra-feminism. Don't just talk about liberation, be liberated. And somehow that icon of female oppression became a symbol of freedom and dominance.'

'Really?' Plant said.

'Oh well, maybe it was all about the money.'

'What, junkies fucking for a fix.'

'No, no, no,' Mac said. 'High-end stuff. Canberra. Politicians. Diplomats. Rock stars.'

'Politicians are high-end, you're saying?'

'Company directors, then,' Mac said. 'What's the difference? They all become company directors after they've qualified for their parliamentary pensions.'

'And you're saying she wrote about it?'

'I think she might have. Or a magazine piece. Not the sort of thing I remember.'

'I thought you remembered everything.'

‘You do so flatter a fellow,’ Mac said.

‘I do my best.’

‘Not good enough,’ Mac said. ‘You make no remark on my themed music.’

Mac always had music playing, varying in its degree of obtrusiveness. George Butterworth’s setting of *A Shropshire Lad* resonated hauntingly.

‘Tell me.’

‘All settings of literary texts,’ Mac said proudly, gesturing vaguely towards the speakers mounted on the walls. ‘Why did I never think of it before? Haydn’s *Creation*. Did you know the libretto is an English translation of a German translation of the English of *Paradise Lost*?’

‘No, I didn’t,’ Plant admitted.

‘And then there’s Britten’s *The Turn of the Screw*. Puccini’s *La Bohème*. The possibilities are endless.’

‘And you’ll have the said literary texts on display for sale.’

‘What a splendid idea! I never dreamt you were so wise in the ways of retail. How could I have failed to think of it myself?’

‘Should keep you quiet for a while.’

‘Busy, perhaps, but not quiet,’ Mac said, turning up the volume.

As he turned to leave Plant noticed copies of *Billy Budd* and *A Shropshire Lad* placed prominently on the counter.

‘How about *Oliver*?’ he suggested. ‘Or *The Phantom of the Opera*, maybe?’

‘I’ll get them in for next time you call,’ Mac promised, unfazed, ‘along with *Cats*.’

He probably would. The whole thing had the potential of a magnificent obsession.

Back in Claire’s apartment, Plant examined his purchase. *What I Did and How, When and Why I Did It* was a collection of short pieces. Stories. Or reminiscences. There was a careful ambiguity about it. Nowhere did it say it was fiction and nowhere did it say it was autobiography. He turned it round, front cover, back cover. No reviews with credits to major media, it was her first book, how could there be? It was quite a slim volume, 128 pages, from the days when slim volumes still had a cachet. Maybe they were all the stories that she had written and the publisher had been happy to do a slim volume since it would cost less to produce than a fat volume, or even a medium-sized volume. Couldn't say average-size volume since the average size changed according to marketing strategies, blockbusters the norm one year, trilogies the next, or whatever. 192 pages used to be the basic norm in the days when books were printed in sixteen or thirty-two-page sections. What a wealth of arcane information he found he possessed when it came to it, Plant reflected. Almost archaeological. He looked at the text, monotype, linotype, offset, filmset, IBM composer. He used to be able to tell, but he was not sure that he could any more. All those varieties of book production. All those years of change. This capacity to drift into reverie needed to be controlled, he realized. That it was technological reverie rather than erotic fantasy made no difference. That the two were becoming interchangeable was a worry in itself. But the basic worry was the potential to slip away from the issue in hand. Literally in hand.

He turned back to the book he was holding. The stories or episodes themselves were all in the first person, which suggested memoir. But the first-person narrators all had different names. Annabel, Belinda, Carla, Dianne, Evelyn, Frances, Gillian, Hillary, Ivana, Jennifer, Kate, Lucy, Mabel, Nona... It would have been easy enough to have standardized the names and had all the episodes related by the same person. Indeed, the book might have started out that way, Plant speculated, and the names changed from episode to episode only afterwards, from some editorial anxiety. Or something more subtle than anxiety, some attempt to raise the possibility that all the events had happened to one person and that they were all in fact true and that that one person was the author: but if the names changed from story to story that couldn't be the case, could it? Or could it? With that contrived alphabetization signalling something. Clever marketing ploy, perhaps. Like the title. Which had a certain attention-attracting modishness that was immediately lost when the book was inevitably and routinely catalogued and listed by its short title, *What I Did*, which didn't do anything for sales or promotion.

There was the story about travelling and arriving at some Mediterranean destination with no hotel booking and not much cash and finding a cafe and a likely looking man on his own whom she contrived to be picked up by and spend the rest of the week with at his very comfortable accommodation. And the next week across the Adriatic and more of the same. Then there was the Sydney story, drunken night out, picking up the waiter at the restaurant and taking him home only to find she'd made an arrangement with some other male she was having a scene with and he was waiting in her bed for her, so after something of a carry-on she ended up screwing both of them. The media magnate story was a suggestive one, if you speculated who the magnate might be, with his penchant for dinner at home with a couple or so more or less naked chicks and an assortment of hard drugs and the magnate firing off his collection of firearms at the chandeliers by way of having a good time. It seemed to be some sort of regular arrangement, thirteenth of each month or something. But the incident of the girl being raffled as the prize at a football club dinner was apparently a one-off, fun as it seemed to have been.

They were good stories. Good enough, anyway, to keep on reading them, not heavy going, not at all turgid, the narrative such as it was skipping along with a carefree exhilaration. And the enigmatic, erotic uncertainty, is that really what happened, did you really, is that how it was, or was that something someone else told you, did you do it or did you just hear about it or did you hear about it and go and try it out for yourself? Or they could all have been made up. Pure fiction. Of that artist as heroine attention-seeking variety. Don't look at my works, ye mighty, just look at me.

He browsed through *What I Did* until the light began to fade. Then he went out and walked up to Military Road and found a noodle bar. He bought a takeaway stir-fried vegetarian rice noodles and tofu. Back in the apartment he went into his bedroom, dug out one of the foils that Fullalove had prepared and went back into the kitchen, put it in a saucepan, covered it with water, and let it boil for fifteen minutes. He sat looking at the panoramic view of the city as he ate the dope and the noodles, the lights in the apartment blocks and office buildings, the corporate signs high on the tops of the tower blocks, the dark expanse of the harbour and the lights of the ferries criss-crossing it. They brought back to mind one of the poets of the city, Kenneth Slessor, and his celebrations of the lights and the harbour and the good times, and his lament for the drunken cartoonist Joe Lynch fallen overboard into the dark night.

Chapter Six

Claire phoned up. Plant was sitting back with *What I Did* in hand, enjoying the panoramic views through the windows and the book-lined walls in between. The books were not totally lined up to the ceiling and spilling out over the floor like Fullalove's shrine to paranoia. Not stacked on the floor and doubled up on the shelves. But accessible. And literary. Not the Kraft-Ebbing and Marx and Havelock Ellis and Chairman Mao that Fullalove favoured. But Katherine Mansfield and Thomas Hardy and Christina Stead and Willa Cather and suchlike. They exuded traces of a civilization, a dying one maybe, but nothing visibly decaying. Which was more than could be said of Fullalove's necropolis of the printed word with its stained and silverfish-eaten pages, cracked glue, broken spines, mildewed covers.

'Just checking to see if you'd arrived and if everything was all right.'

'No problems,' he said. He could have said 'Perfect' or 'Splendid' or something equally enthusiastic. But it was an employer-employee relationship. He didn't want to give the impression everything was idyllic and he was onto a good deal. He was working, after all. He wasn't down in Sydney on a holiday, he needed to keep that clear.

'How are you getting on?' she asked.

'I've been reading one of her books.'

'Oh,' she said, 'don't feel you have to. I know she's my sister. But really. Why would you?'

'I don't know. You asked me if I'd ever read her.'

'Did I? Sorry about that. I wasn't putting any pressure on you.'

'No, no problem. It's quite interesting.'

'Really? Which one is that.'

'*What I Did and...*'

'Oh, that one. That was the first one. It's hard to find, I'm amazed you got hold of it. It never really sold. A book of short stories by a first-time author. You know. I don't think they even remaindered it, they just pulped it. So there aren't that many copies around. It was never reprinted.'

So much for the publishing history. But there was the matter of content.

'Fascinating reading,' Plant said.

'Really? Oh, I suppose so.'

'Gives an interesting picture,' he said. He tried to sound casual, unconcerned. 'Are they based on her experience or...?'

She groaned.

'That's what every male who ever reads them asks.'

'Sorry to be so predictable.'

'Predictable!' she said. 'Just voyeuristic.'

'Well, they do make you wonder.'

'You, maybe,' she said.

'But not you.'

'No.'

'Why's that?' he asked. 'Because you know they are true, or you know they're not?'

'I don't know,' she said. 'They could all be true. They could all be fiction. Or they could be a bit of both. What do you think?'

Plant did not know what to think. Not an unfamiliar situation.

'Are there any more?' he asked.

'More what?'

'Stories. Like these.'

She gave another groan, more of a grunt this time.

'You're getting a taste for them?'

'No, no, not at all.'

'You're shocked?'

'No.'

'Turned on.'

'No.'

'Aroused.'

'No.'

'Turned off.'

'Not at all.'

She laughed at him.

'I wondered if she carried on in this...'

'Vein? Sewer? Genital tract?' she offered.

'If she published a follow-up.'

'No. She'd already given up poetry, no money in it. Then she turned to stories and that market all dried up. When she started out, back then, people still used to write short stories. But gradually all the magazines folded or they stopped publishing fiction, and publishers didn't like collections of stories, that was clear from the way they treated hers. So she moved on.'

'So she was into the money.'

'Money and fame, yes. Cash and celebrity.'

'So this *What I Did* could all have been commercial calculation, or miscalculation, rather than true confessions.'

'Could be. Or both.'

'Not a commitment to art.'

'Heavens no. The only art Liz was interested in was her own artfulness. She wanted to be out there, up there. Herself. Poetry, stories, travel, lectures, it was all about her. She was the focus. Forget art.'

'And the stories were never reprinted,' he checked again.

'No. Didn't sell.'

'Didn't she ever try to get them reprinted later? When she'd made a name.'

'Not that I ever heard.'

'Or did she suppress them?'

'I don't know. She could have. If she felt they were a liability. Or it could just be no one was interested. How about that? That would be pretty devastating, wouldn't it? Do a full-frontal nudity display and no one bothers to look.'

'Do I detect a note of satisfaction?' Plant asked.

'Do you?' she asked.

'So the book wasn't a great success.'

'It didn't become a best-seller, if that's what you mean. But it got her started. So people who knew sort of knew about her. And she got work on the magazines.'

'What magazines?'

'I can't remember their names.'

'How did she get it?'

'I've no idea.'

'Through bonking that media magnate?'

'Who do you mean?'

'The one in that story.'

'I don't know about that.'

'But it's not impossible.'

'No, not impossible.'

'Were they magazines that he published that she wrote for?'

'Could have been. But I don't know how hands-on he was.'

'Sounds like his hands were on whatever he could grab.'

'Sexually, no doubt. But I don't know how he ran his business.'

'How else would she have got published?'

'I imagine she wrote things that they thought worth publishing. I think she'd got to know one of the editors somehow.'

'And then?'

'And then she was off.'

'And you?'

'Me? I just carried on as I usually did. I didn't have her great ambitions.'

'Did you miss hanging out with her?'

'We were sisters.'

'But doing stuff together...'

'What are you insinuating?' she asked. Somewhat sharply, Plant felt.

'Insinuating? What do you mean?'

'What do *you* mean, more to the point? No, Plant, while you lie back visualizing Liz in her prime at orgy after dope-fest after Sodom and Gomorrah, just leave me out of the picture. I never fitted into that world.'

'That world?'

'Her world. Don't try and imagine what I looked like then, what I wore or didn't wear. Just leave me out of the picture. Like I wasn't there. Like I wasn't. So don't imagine I ever was.'

She seemed somewhat adamant about it.

'Fair enough,' Plant said.

Chapter Seven

The Liz Lambastier papers were in the Mitchell Library collection in the New South Wales State Library. Plant decided to make an occasion of it and enjoy the available delights of Sydney, starting with the harbour. He took a bus to the ferry wharf and a ferry across to Circular Quay, the Opera House framing the perspective one side, a huge cruise ship moored at the Overseas Terminal framing the other, and the great steel girders of the Harbour Bridge arching up into the sky, all very dramatic and sun-drenched and contributing to a generally good mood which he welcomed and appreciated as he walked up Macquarie Street, past the old colonial sandstone buildings on the right, preserved facades with concrete high-rises rising high above them, past the road leading down to the old VD clinic, and on the other side the Conservatorium of Music and the Botanic Gardens and then the proud portico of the NSW State Library, a mature-aged Shakespeare marooned amidst the traffic flow on his own Prospero's island before it, Falstaff, Othello, Portia, Romeo and Juliet milling around at his feet.

The size of the Lambastier collection was daunting. The catalogue indicated something like two-hundred boxes, not yet catalogued. It made sense that Claire hadn't wanted to search through all that herself. Unwelcome memories unwilling to be revived, maybe; or just a recoil from the sheer bulk of the collection. Maybe not, who knew? All he knew was that there was an inordinate amount of material. It had seemed a simple task when she had approached him. But when she approached him he had not known what was involved. Every scrap of correspondence, letters received, postcards, memos, greeting cards, for heaven's sake, Christmas, birthdays, could you believe it? But ah, from famous people. Why else preserve them? International celebrities. Sexually-suggestive invitations from American novelists and British television personalities. Or purportedly so. Who was going to check the handwriting and signatures? Unworthy thoughts, possibly, but provoked by the sheer volume he had to wade through. And the press cuttings. Reviews, mentions. Copy she had written, collected with no apparent system other than comprehensiveness, the same or similar items recurring time and again, maybe they were syndicated articles, but many seemed just to be duplicate or triplicate copies. And the scraps. Folders containing little scraps of paper, torn from little notebooks, the edges frayed where they'd been ripped off the spiral wire-binding, together with receipts from shops, chemists, supermarkets, ATMs, all with notes scribbled on the back, phrases and brief sentences, insights, memory joggers for some paragraph for some article or interview or work in progress.

And the tedium of it. Nothing like a car chase in a crime movie. Though car chases could be pretty tedious, too. But library research is basically just a slow, steady slog. With maybe momentary glimmers of excitement at the discovery that turns out to be a false hope. And the long delays, waiting for boxes to be delivered, only so many boxes allowed out from the stacks at a time. And then leafing through them. Not even reading the contents. To read them would take forever. All he needed to do was to see what was there. There was a box of USBs and he opened them up one by one, checking the titles of the files, opening up the likely ones. There were folders of letters. There were folders of poems. There were typescripts and printouts which just needed to be matched with the published books, in their first and second and third drafts. Though typescripts and printouts, despite their existence in multiple drafts, were a comparatively small proportion of the material. As Claire had said, librarians when they purchased writers' collections, or when they gave a valuation the donor could use for a cultural donations tax deduction, were more interested in correspondence and diaries, in the seedy personal and the potential for gossip, than in the creative product. Plant resisted getting caught up in the diaries and correspondence, at least for the present. He just needed to keep focused on the job in hand, on ascertaining that there was no unpublished manuscript or typescript or printout anywhere around. Everything was neatly filed in folders, labelled, amazingly organized, her side of the story preserved in an amazingly efficient, clerk-like way. Plant wondered whether it was the work of an obsessive, organized, controlling author, preoccupied with posterity, or some efficient assistant. It made things easier, whoever had done it. He was grateful for that. He had dreaded being confronted by a jumble of totally unsorted, muddled papers.

He had been working through the material for a couple of days when, around mid-morning of the third day he became aware of someone standing behind him, behind and to one side, looking over his shoulder at the papers on his desk. He turned his head around and the person moved to the side of the desk, coming into view and standing there rather than passing by.

'Oh, sorry to be looking over your shoulder,' she said, 'but I couldn't help looking.'

Thirty-something female person, long blonde hair, fit-looking figure, wearing gym gear. Maybe not actual gym gear, but the quasi-athletic outfit with its allusion to all that healthy body, vigorous work-out style that young women seemed to favour.

Plant tried his all-purposes smile. Lately he had been working on it, checking himself out when he passed a shop window, consciously shifting his default setting of daily scowl to smile. It came more readily after the ferry ride, a relaxed way to begin the day with its hints of nature, water, spray, seagulls, let alone all the fish and suchlike beneath the surface. The world wasn't such a bad place, he told himself, his mantra. Even if people did choose to wear gym gear. A fine, upstanding lass as they used to say, or write. He couldn't actually remember anyone ever saying it. One of the gym-going generation without a doubt, something Plant not only could not understand but pretty much recoiled from. Racked in a past life, perhaps. No way he was getting tangled up in any of those machines.

But she looked good. Healthy. Vigorous. No obvious hostility or life-threatening menace. Hard to tell with young ladies of a certain age. Or any age. But she seemed safe. Bright eyes, snub nose, and a smile as winning as his own was intended to be.

'Are you working on her?' she asked.

'Yes, sort of,' Plant said.

'Are you writing a book?'

'No, not exactly.'

'Oh,' she said. She seemed neither surprised nor disappointed.

'And you?'

'Me? No, no, it's just that I know someone who was a good friend of hers.'

'Really?' Plant said.

It was quite a lift, a moment of excitement, trudging through the undergrowth of old letters and variant drafts suddenly to encounter a living clue. A connection across the years reinvigorating the stored records with the vibrancy of a living voice. Shall these dead leaves speak? Probably not. But this person standing beside them might. Indeed was already speaking.

A couple of people at neighbouring tables were looking up, which was not just matter of raising eyelids or swivelling pupils, but of stretching, clearing throats, knocking elbows on desktops, shuffling papers and the rest of it in a meaningful, potentially hostile way. Plant looked round at them. They both did. Nothing potential about the hostility, it was unambiguously apparent.

'Do you feel like a coffee?' she asked. 'Do you have time for a break?'

Plant put the lid back on the manuscript box he had open, and stood. He nodded silently. Mouthed a 'Yes'. She led the way out and he followed. Like he was following the thread through the Minotaur's tunnel, trusting it was the right direction.

Chapter Eight

Out in the blazing Sydney sunlight of the library cafe terrace they looked at each other rather blankly. Right, what have you got to say now we're here, who wants to go first?

'Actually,' she said, 'what I really need is a smoke. Do you mind if we walk over to the Domain?'

They went out of the terrace, down past the back of the library and across the road to where the Domain stretched out, grass and trees and joggers and walkers and smokers, dipping down and then rising up to the Art Gallery. He had no strong feelings about smoking, passive or otherwise. The escape from the archives of the dead and departed into the sunlight was relief enough. He felt a sort of compliant happiness, a carefree agreement. The sun, the blue sky, the glittering harbour just down there nearby somewhere, the ambience of literature and achievement and culture, of some sort of meaningfulness and worthwhileness, and an attractive, appealing, smiling companion there, it was like being young in springtime. He didn't need a coffee, it would only give him heartburn and reflux and abdominal distress.

It had its literary associations, the Domain. It featured in fiction. Robert Louis Stevenson and Lloyd Osbourne's *The Wrecker*. William Lane's *The Workingman's Paradise*. Christina Stead's *Seven Poor Men of Sydney*. The place where the unemployed and homeless hung out and slept a century and more ago. 'And what's changed?' Plant heard himself asking, the era of social hope gone and the unemployed and homeless back in force, jobs lost to government free-market policies, homes lost to gambling and alcohol, businesses sanctioned by government, contributing indeed to party political funds, each party as involved as the other in the corruption, the kick-backs, the money-laundering, the facilitation of crime, why does it need the adjective 'organized', but anyway, to the matter in hand, she was an engaging girl, smoking apart, with that capacity to make you feel she was interested in you and your opinions, she could get you to talk, she got Plant to talk, banging on about the homeless and social justice and the good society where politicians and plutocrats would be strung up from every lamp post. He hoped she had not taken him too literally, he didn't want to end up on a terrorist watch list, dangerous to say anything these days. It was just the excitement of finding someone actually seeming to want to listen and he'd got carried away, inventive, exaggerative. He spent his life listening to people and when not listening, watching them or checking up on them in some way. Like now, even, checking up on the dead, where's your missing manuscript? So to have a chance to talk to someone, to hold forth, to be listened to was something rare. The people he knew best all wanted to be listened to, insisted on it, talked over you, ground you down. It was a struggle to be with them, trying to get equal time, grabbing the microphone as it were. Anyway. Here he was. Being listened to while she puffed away at a cigarette. Rare these days. Listening or smoking.

'You're an academic, then,' she said, when he finally stopped.

'No, not me.'

'Oh, I thought if you were writing on Liz...'

'No,' he said again.

'But you're writing something about her.'

'I'm not, actually,' he said. Maybe he should. Maybe he should make a career change and use his research and investigative skills to become a biographer. Or a literary critic, except he couldn't see much future in that. Not from current projections.

'So what are you?' she asked. She did it in the best winsome manner. If winsome was the word. Challenging and cheeky. Pert, if you wanted to take it that way, rather than intrusive and interrogative.

'I'm a researcher.'

‘Oh,’ she said. Then, ‘Why?’

‘A chap’s got to earn a living,’ he said.

She smiled again. Someone else might have been offended at his uncooperativeness. Or asked point-blank what he was up to. But she smiled, probably not especially sweetly, but still a smile.

‘You should meet my aunt,’ she said.

At least it wasn’t you should meet my mother, one of those sentences from far back, childhood, adolescence, something evoking a frisson of resistance, a paralysis of fear. No, I’d rather not meet your mother, or your father for that matter. But an aunt?

‘Why’s that?’ he asked.

‘You might find her useful.’

‘In what way?

‘In whatever you’re looking for.’

She drew on her cigarette. Plant had nothing to fiddle with, not even the coffee that had been promised and then withdrawn, delayed maybe, certainly not there now.

How do you know I’m looking for something? he might have asked, but didn’t. It was requiring all his focus and concentration, saying nothing to this attractive, snub nosed female person, wallowing in the sun and her smiles and playing silly buggers in not telling her what he was up to. He was obviously up to something, otherwise he wouldn’t have been working through Lambastier’s papers. It was only his automatic suspicion that she might be up to something too that was making him evasive. Apart from his natural evasiveness. And after all, if he was seriously looking for a missing manuscript, why not let people know he was? After all, this might be the amazing serendipity that scholars always went on about, the crucial information being deposited in your lap by happy chance. But he was standing there not sitting, nothing could be deposited in his lap. He looked at her. Pretty obviously she could be up to something, and if she wasn’t it didn’t matter. Having established that, he could move on to the next step.

‘Would she want to meet me?’ he asked.

‘Who?’

It had been a long time between sentences.

'Your aunt.'

'Of course. She'd be thrilled. She'd love to talk to you about Liz.'

'And what about you?'

'What about me?'

'Would you like to talk to me about Liz?'

She looked at him strangely. It was all sounding a bit strange, even to Plant, no stranger to the strange.

'Isn't that what we're doing now?' she asked.

'What?'

'Talking about Liz.'

She smiled. Winningly, as they used to put it.

'I suppose we are,' he agreed, though he hadn't heard much of any substance. 'Did you know her?'

'She was like a wicked aunt,' she said. 'Even wickeder than my own wicked aunt who she used to visit. I used to see her there.'

'Wicked?'

'You know. Like wicked uncles. They'd always slip you a present. Bring you things people disapproved of.'

'What sort of things?'

'Chocolate and stuff.'

'Oh.'

'You thought condoms and cocaine and black diamonds.'

'Not exactly.'

'She'd blow in from wherever she'd been travelling and bring these amazing things. All these exotic things from places she'd been to.'

'Really,' he said, a default response of a researcher and investigator that he had not attempted to reprogram. 'What sort of things?'

'Oh, you know.'

He didn't. He'd once been given a dead piranha, and another time a Niugini carving of someone or other with an enlarged penis. Gigantically enlarged.

'Bracelets. Necklaces. Beautiful fabrics. Not massively expensive. At least I don't think they were. But always beautiful. And unique. No one else ever had anything like them.'

Gewgaws he might have said except he'd never been sure how to pronounce it. Them. And anyway, it sounded too dismissive.

'So you looked forward to her visits.'

'You bet.'

'And they were frequent?'

'The visits? I've no idea. I was only a kid.'

'Did you keep in touch afterwards?'

'After what?'

'After you were no longer a kid.'

'I'm still a kid at heart,' she said, laughing.

He waited.

'Yes, I'd see her once in a while. She was always fun. Good company. And interesting. She always had interesting stories.'

'About what?'

'Oh, adventures on her travels. People she'd met. The usual stuff.'

He nodded. Wisely. Knowingly. In agreement.

'You never said what your interest in her is,' she said.

He tried for the casual note. 'Didn't I?'

'No, you didn't.'

If she was up to something, then she was up to something. There was no way of avoiding it. Better to find out what she was up to. If anything. In which case he might as well tell her what he was up to. It might be a way of finding the manuscript, whether she was up to something or not. It was a lead and so far he hadn't had any others.

He took out his wallet and removed a card. Research assistance, investigative reporting. He gave it to her.

'I'm looking to see if there's an unpublished manuscript of hers in her papers.'

'Why?'

'Why? With a view to getting it published, presumably.'

'Presumably? Don't you know?'

He shrugged.

'Theirs not to reason why,' he offered.

'Who asked you to look?'

'Can't say, sorry. Client confidentiality.'

'What, a publisher? An agent?'

'Something like that.'

'But you can't tell me.'

He shook his head.

'How mean,' she said.

He apologized.

'Sorry, it's just the way the business works.'

'The business?'

'My business.'

'Are you some kind of private investigator?'

'Just a researcher.'

'Why should I believe you?'

'No reason.'

'At least that's an honest response.'

'If you say so.'

She looked at him, one of those hard, keen looks, and laughed.

He laughed with her, as convincingly as he could. He could feel her assessing the insincerity of it.

'What's the manuscript about?'

'I don't know.'

'You don't know.'

'No. It may not even exist. I'm just looking to see if there is anything anywhere.'

'Anywhere?'

'If it's not with her papers here.'

'So where would it be if not here?'

'That's what I was hired to find out.'

'So it could be anywhere.'

'If it exists, yes.'

'Like in an old trunk forgotten in an attic.'

The shafts of sunlight through the dormer windows reflecting off the dust.

'A distinct possibility. Or an indistinct one, maybe.'

'Or in the hands of a deranged private collector.'

'Couldn't have put it better myself.'

'So you've got yourself quite a job, Mr...'

She looked at the card he had given her.

'Mr Plant.'

'That's the name of the game.'

'What name?' she asked.

He smiled.

'What game?'

He smiled some more.

She trampled out the remains of her cigarette on the grass.

'We shall meet again, Mr Plant, never fear. I'll give you a call when my aunt can see you.'

'Thank you,' he said. 'That's very kind of you.'

'My pleasure,' she said, not unenigmatically.

'I look forward to it,' he said, no less ambiguously.

They walked back to the terrace cafe and Plant went to order himself an English breakfast tea and whatever she might want. But she carried on down the walkway to Macquarie Street. She waved, and disappeared. Had she finished whatever work she had been doing in the library? Had she been doing any work there at all? He hadn't seen her at a desk when he had arrived, nor when he was ordering things. He hadn't noticed her at all till she came and stood beside him.

The gym gear and the smoking puzzled him. Weren't the two contradictory? But what was wrong with contradictions? So what if I contradict myself, I contain multitudes, as Walt Whitman put it. Was it actually gym gear, for that matter, or simply fashion? And what did it denote, either way? That she exuded health? It had never been the sort of thing Plant had made a point of looking for. Was it to let men, and women too, know that she was no easy pushover? That she could give you a run for your money? It was all too close to the school gym, that site of horror and torment, for Plant. But clearly some folk loved the association. Maybe she was off to the gym now, exercise after library work, assuming she'd done any. And that glowing, potentially yielding softness that had lured him out into the Domain now hardening into protein-packed muscle, steroid-enhanced sinew, hormone-fed flesh, the whole like a medical research project financed by the health police and the military. He took his tea and sat in the sun for a while, sipping and reflecting and coming to no clear conclusions, before he went back inside to the cool reading room and the quiet and the turning of pages of past days, past lives.

There was no unpublished manuscript amongst the papers. There were draft versions of various published books. There were the folders of correspondence. There were scraps of notes bundled together but they were just brief paragraphs, sometimes just sentences, sometimes paragraphs, scribbled down in notebooks and ripped out and preserved, but nothing sustained, nothing of any substance. This was all material that had been gone through and probably culled, work that had been finished and dealt with and published. But there were no works in progress, no manuscripts broken off, no half-completed memoirs or fragmentary essays, none of the usual detritus of a writer's desk. If there had been a work in progress she had kept it with her to work on when she had deposited the papers. What she had deposited here she had finished with.

Chapter Nine

Amongst Lambastier's papers there had been several versions of her curriculum vitae, updated over the years. It saved him from having to look her up online. No need to provide electronic evidence of his current enquiries. She listed a BA (Hons) degree from his own university, so he phoned his supervisor from those days. The obvious way to begin assembling some background information that hadn't been sifted and selected by Lambastier herself. Or at least an easy way.

Dennis was as eager to have lunch as ever. Some people as they got older got less sociable, found sitting still at a restaurant table for more than twenty minutes insupportable, skipped the desert which they weren't supposed to eat anyway, and rushed off clutching their phones claiming some other engagement which they probably didn't have, sustaining a conversation just too hard. Not so Dennis. After forty years of holding forth in lectures and tutorials, the need to have someone to talk to was entrenched and embedded and clearly still satisfying. He was always glad to converse, theorize, pontificate, adjudicate, enthuse and despair. More despair than enthusiasm these latter days. But he had always been open to despair at the ways of the world. Not personally. It was despair at the ways of the world that kept him happy, a constant source of malign satisfaction that everything predicted was coming true and in the end the whole system would collapse and the sooner the better.

Dennis suggested yum cha in the inner west. His days of going into the city were long passed, only executives and politicians and city councillors and the mayor with designated parking facilities drove into the city any more. Now it was all cycle tracks and tram tracks and no parking and keep out. 'Stripped of our citizenship by arbitrary decree,' as Dennis put it.

Plant was unsure whether Dennis was more dangerous prodding the air with chopsticks, chilli sauce dripping off their tips, than with the knife and fork of other eateries. The trick was to sit well back and not lean forward to hear what he was saying. Lean back and lip-read. Most of what he said he repeated anyway, a practice from those years of university lecturing, making sure every point was made three times.

Dangerous or not, Dennis seemed to be well known at the yum cha place. And accepted. Presumably he hadn't stabbed anyone in the eye or nostril with his chopsticks. The waitress made a point of offering him chicken feet, a broad grin as he waved her away. Nothing daunted, next time round she offered tripe, delighted to provoke his recoil. Ritual jokes over, she returned with garlic chives, snow peas and spinach dumplings. All wholesomely vegetarian as long as you disregarded the little prawns amidst the vegetables. Plant disregarded them. Dennis asked for a second chilli sauce dish so they didn't have to share the same one, dipping their partially eaten dumplings into it.

'Liz Lambastier, why are you interested in her?'

'Did you know her?'

'Know her? Who didn't? A nightmare. An absolute fucking nightmare.'

'The operative word being...'

'Ha ha,' Dennis said. 'Yes, I suppose I could have fucked her. Might have. Well, we could have fucked each other, heaven forbid any implication of male dominance, far indeed from it. Not impossible. More than that I'm not prepared to say. Not in these witch-hunting days. Except that I was the one being harassed, let's get that clear. And I wouldn't have been the only one. Oh, she was all right, just a nightmare, clearly fiendishly ambitious but that wasn't apparent at the time, I mean it was probably just par for the course, everyone of that age in that university milieu was fiendishly ambitious, we wouldn't have been there otherwise, we were at the peak of the competitive system, so even if we didn't recognize it, we were. Ambitious,' he added, in case it had got lost.

'As the Nobel laureate puts it, she'd been with the professors, and they'd liked her looks,' he intoned. 'Cut a swathe through the male population. You might have thought it was just sex. I imagine we all thought it was, just sex. But it could've been she was targeting potentially useful figures and fucking them, could be this was a groupie motivation, or could be what they call networking now. Or maybe she was just looking for material to write about. "Everything I do is for my art," that old line. Still, it's a good line. It's worked before so why not use it again? Fine for writers. Doesn't quite work for scholars. Shame about that, I always felt. She wasn't a scholar, anyway. Bright enough. Can't remember if she did graduate work. Probably did, started it anyway, a way to get a living-allowance. But what she was going for was the literary celebrity business. A good time for a woman. And she was one of the women the times got.'

'You don't like her,' Plant suggested.

'Well...'

'You never liked her.'

'No, no, it's not that. It's knowing what I know now, and believing what I believe, and a lifetime's inevitable observation of people like her, students, colleagues, and the whole cultural, political scene, I'm wary. At least I am now. At the time, when we were all young and some of us were innocent, everything looked different. Everything looked possible, for one thing. You could make things happen, and things did happen, all the time. Books, magazines, alternative papers, theatre, movies. So much was happening you never had time to question it, you were flat out absorbing and responding to it and creating and commenting on this vibrant new world. So someone like Liz was just what you got to expect on the scene. Bossy, pushy, energetic, self-confident and at the same time fragile, wounded, insecure. There were a whole lot like her. They start off all winsome and willing and nubile and you help them, help them get published or whatever and in no time at all they've turned into hard-nosed career women. You kept out of their way in the end. At least I did. Saw her in the staff club bar one time with one of our fêted, state-sponsored writers. She smiled, wanly. So I smiled wanly back and ducked round the corner and drank down my beer and didn't hang around. Sad really,' he added.

'She got herself in all the right places. She must have worked hard at it. Or had a bit of help on the way. She wasn't just hanging around for the parties. Some judicious fucking, no doubt. Poems in that anthology of women's poetry. Or so she said. I never actually checked. Not my area, as we used to say. Well, it wasn't. Not any more. The literary arena was being turned into a feminist space. People like her were on a roll. Mere males were markedly unwelcome. So out paths never afterwards crossed. Not after she became famous.'

'What did she become famous for?' Plant asked.

'For being famous, maybe? Who knows? At some point it is decreed they shall become famous, and famous they become.'

'She went for the literary celebrity business, you said.'

'Did I?'

'Yes.'

'I suppose it's true. I don't honestly know what she went for. But she started off in the poetry scene, I remember that. She was up to her ears in the poetry wars.'

'The poetry wars?' Plant said. 'What were they?'

'The way I look at it,' Dennis said, 'is they were a cross between a schoolyard brawl and a Cold War confrontation.'

Plant tried to envisage it, but failed. Dennis spelled it out. The civil war between the poets arose from a dispute over the control of a poetry magazine. It was in one aspect a fight between a couple of generations. You couldn't say it was between the traditionalists and the modernists because each side claimed to be both at various times. Whenever it suited them. But while one gang was flying the flag of Dylan Thomas and Ted Hughes, the other had signed up for Allen Ginsberg and the Beats, American modernism and postmodernism. Proxy wars, in effect, the confrontation of European and American culture, fought out beneath Australian skies.

'So what were the issues?'

'Issues?'

'Grounds for the dispute.'

'Oh, modernization. Being up to date.'

'Modernization?'

'Sure, seizing control of the magazine and Americanizing it.'

'Why?'

'On the grounds that it was out of touch.'

'Out of touch with what?'

'With what people were writing.'

'And after the takeover?'

'Just a new aesthetic.'

'Postmodernism.'

'Pretty much.'

'And she was writing that sort of thing.'

'No idea. Can't remember what she was writing. But over all it was all pretty abstract.'

'Abstract Expressionism.'

'That sort of thing. You know, high modernism.'

'So not about social issues and imperialist wars and so on.'

'No way. This was pure poetry.'

'And that's what they fought about?'

'You've said it.'

Plant dipped his dim sim into the chilli sauce. It all seemed very remote.

'The standard of discourse was primary school,' Dennis said. 'Low-level personal abuse, ageist prejudice and shit-kicking just for the hell of it. They were hardly out of kindergarten, pretty well still teenagers, poncing and preening around like they were God's gift to creativity. Quarrelling over who got to run a poetry magazine was just an alternative to getting pissed or getting stoned or pursuing sexual opportunities. Not even an alternative. Something to carry on with simultaneously. Just having a good time.'

'You were there?' Plant asked.

'I was around. Not being a poet, thank heavens, I wasn't involved in it. But I had colleagues who were.'

'At the university?'

'The only colleagues I can lay claim to.'

'And they were involved?'

'The ones who felt themselves involved in American literature were.'

'American.'

'Of course. Agents of influence. It was all part of the American cultural mission. Save the world from socialist realism.'

'It sounds a bit extreme.'

'Extreme times, extreme situations. The CIA gets involved, you've got to believe it.'

'How were they involved? In a poetry magazine?'

'Back then there was a State Department plan to tour an exhibition of Abstract Expressionist paintings around the world. Show the world that America was at the cutting edge of the visual arts. No more boring representation. No more tractors and power lines. Just squiggles and smudges. Anyway, Congress wouldn't agree to fund it; they figured this was all decadent, indulgent crap so they said no, forget it. So the CIA was called in to fund it secretly.'

'Really?'

'Would I tell a lie?'

'And this happened?'

'Sure did. And it worked. Everyone goes "Wow, wham, bam, American art, the future."'

'But this was visual art.'

'Same thing applied to poets pretty obviously. We had the whole ABC of them sent out here, Ashbery, Bly, Creeley, Duncan... Send Ginsberg round the world and save the planet.'

'You're saying they were CIA?'

'Not necessarily. And not necessarily consciously. But the programme to drown the world with American cultural production was undoubtedly a CIA one. Or CIA assisted. Via the United States Information Service.'

'And you're saying the poetry wars were part of that operation.'

'I would've thought so,' Dennis said.

'Interesting.'

'Come on, you can do better than that. "Interesting" – how pathetic. "Devastating" would be more appropriate.'

'Really?'

'As a piece of cultural imperialism.'

'I guess so.'

'You can only guess. We're so saturated in these values now no one can imagine anything else. Can you?'

'Can I what?'

'Can you imagine a different cultural landscape? You can't. We've been totally taken over.'

Plant had no reply. Nothing that would be acceptable or adequate. He sat there, silent.

'So you're saying that all these poets and magazine people were American special forces on a mission,' he said after a while.

'Agents of influence. Objectively, yes. But not necessarily consciously.'

'Collaborators.'

'Without perhaps realizing the full extent of what they were collaborating in. They just wanted to be new. The future. Shake off the colonial past and all the old repressive values.'

'Sounds fair enough.'

'And introduce the new economic and cultural imperialism and the new repressive values.'

'And your colleagues mixed up in this, what were they at?'

'They were besotted by the American.'

'Why?'

'Maybe they were rejected by the British. Couldn't get a Commonwealth Scholarship. Felt their faces would never fit at Oxbridge.'

'So they did their graduate work in the States?'

'Some of them. Some just wrote on American Lit for their graduate work here.'

'As opposed to writing on English Lit.'

'Or Aus Lit.'

'So it wasn't an Australian independence assertion, shaking off the shackles of the cultural cringe.'

'They might have thought it was. The height of Australianism then as now being imitative Americanism.'

'A bit savage, isn't it?'

'I feel a bit savage,' Dennis said. 'More than a bit. As I see the world I grew up in reduced to rubble.'

'Though not literally.'

'Not like Vietnam or Iraq or Libya or Syria, maybe. Not in terms of bricks and mortar.'

'And human lives.'

'And human lives. But in cultural degradation, it's been catastrophic.'

'And you blame the poets.'

'No, I don't blame them. Father forgive them for they know not what they do. But between them, the poets and my colleagues and the arts administrators, they carpet-bombed and defoliated and poisoned a whole living tradition. Or tried to. They can't win ultimately, of course. History will prove them wrong.'

'That's something,' Plant said, though not with any deep conviction.

'You have to preserve hope. But in the meantime...'

'In the meantime?'

'Look at it,' Dennis said. 'Listen to it. Read it, if you can find anything you can bear to read any more. All that tired old junk they foisted on us. How we used to struggle to read that so-called modernist shit they used to promote. Mallarmé, Baudelaire, Rimbaud. These be your Gods, oh Israel. And all that dreary formalist stuff New Directions used to publish. At least City Lights had a bit of anarchistic life. Though all of it objectively reactionary. Non-cooperative, individualistic, look-at-me preening, I'm an artist, with no redeeming social or moral message.'

'You advocate moral messages now you've retired?'

'When I have to deal with this Americanized promotion of the dregs of European decadence, yes.'

'You're sure you're not getting a bit extreme?'

'Probably. Why not? It was an extreme situation and we've inherited the consequences. They killed off art and culture and morality in one...'

He tailed off.

'One fell swoop, as they used to say?' Plant offered.

'One orgiastic generation.'

'Ah, blame the young.'

'No, pity the young, we were the victims. This was foisted on us. To bring on the decadence.'

'And you bought it.'

'Oh yes. Bought is the word. They weren't doing it for free. It was all about money and profit and the perpetuation of the inequitable distribution of wealth. Never doubt it for one moment.'

'Does it still exist?'

'What?'

'The poetry magazine they fought over.'

'No. Died years ago.'

'So what was the point of the takeover if it didn't keep going?'

'Kill off the opposition.'

'Opposition?'

'Opposition to American so-called values. It may not have been a big operation. There may never have been any plans to keep it going. Just another piece of state-sponsored terrorism. Take out any groups that provide a focus for resistance. Cultural, religious, political, whatever. Take it over and wipe it out. It's just like big business. Take over the rival brands and close them down. You see it all the time in publishing.'

'So what's your interest in all this?' Dennis asked. 'You writing the cultural history of the client state?'

'I'm trying to find a missing manuscript.'

'Ah, the old purloined letter number. Whose manuscript?'

'Liz Lambastier's.'

'Probably on display in a showcase in the Jessie Street National Women's Library.'

'No, it isn't. I've already checked.'

Dennis grunted. 'She didn't write that many, did she? Got a lot of exposure on a handful of books. Barely a handful. Funny how it works. There are people who plug on and on, writing book after book, and they hardly get a look in. And dear Liz writes a couple of travellers' tales and she gets acclaim and accolades and all the rest of it.'

'The travel books were popular, apparently.'

'Were they? I didn't keep up. Not my area. So what's the missing manuscript?'

'I don't know.'

'More travel? Memoir?'

'Could be. Could be a memoir, could be a novel.'

'Same difference. All about Liz. How do you know it exists?'

'I don't for sure. Her sister thinks it does.'

'And what's her angle?'

'She wants me to try and find it.'

'So she can burn it?'

'She didn't say.'

'You didn't ask.'

'No, I didn't imagine at the time that burning it might be part of the plan.'

'Well, now you can.'

'Why would she want to burn it?'

'Because it says nasty things about the sister or the family. Because it records sexual exploits that might bring shame on the good name of the Lambastiers. Because it records extreme drug use or sexual exploitation of the young.'

'I guess it's a possibility.'

'Of course it is.'

'I assumed she probably wanted to publish it if it was any good.'

'So what if she plans to burn it?'

'Not my business what gets done with it.'

'Oh, Plant, that you would condone the destruction of cultural artefacts.'

'You're saying I shouldn't now. Her work should be preserved. That's not the impression I got a moment ago.'

'Never mind the quality, think of the incriminating potential. It's all evidence for future cultural historians. Let alone for contemporary warlock hunters.'

'What incriminating potential? Kill her for her bad verses?'

'Could be the kiss-and-tell memoir we've been waiting for.'

'Have you?'

'Haven't we all?'

'Is that so?'

'In fear and trembling. You'd have to consider it a possibility. With someone like her. It could be a minefield. She could have named names. All the embarrassing, humiliating details of all the men in her life. And women too for that matter.'

'Assuming the manuscript exists and assuming it's a memoir.'

'Always look on the dark side,' Dennis said. 'It prepares you for the worst.'

Nonetheless the waitress came round with custard tarts, shining fresh and golden like the midday sun. She offered them to Dennis. He nodded acceptance vigorously.

'Got to have some pleasures.'

Plant agreed.

'So, looking on the dark side, what dark secrets about you is Lambastier likely to reveal?'

'I doubt that she'd remember me,' Dennis said. 'Not in print. I'm not one of the names she'd want to drop. Never made it into the glitterati. Thank the Lord. There are some books you're glad not to find your name in. But I can't say I care one way or the other. Not worried about my citation index now I'm retired. Never was, to tell the truth.'

'Citation index?'

'Just another of those American monitoring set-ups where they listed all the references to your work that other academics had made. Surveillance disguised as career enhancement.'

'They?'

'American scientists mainly. They seem to believe in numbers rather than substance. The more you get mentioned the better you are deemed to be. Forget whether you ever say anything worth saying.'

'So if she mentioned you it would be recorded there.'

'Not if it isn't published. And I doubt it would be recorded anyway. They just note references to academic articles.'

'Not mentions in memoirs.'

'Not that I know of. Though who knows, there might be some secret operation like the Umpteen Days of the Condor reading everything. Anyway, who cares? I can't see the vice-chancellor calling for my retrospective removal for gross moral turpitude. There'd be a statute of limitations anyway, wouldn't there? Surely. Anyway, I'm not going to sweat on it. Can't see that anybody would care that much. Might sell a few copies if she lists everyone she ever fucked. The trick is not to provide an index. Then you can't just turn to the back to see if you're mentioned. You have to read the whole bloody book, can't do that standing in a bookshop. Not for four or five hours. Have to buy the bloody thing and comb through it at leisure. And you don't even know it exists, you say, and it certainly hasn't been published. It's not like I'm a clergyman or a choirmaster or a swimming coach or something. Consenting heterosexual adults and all that. Though that may be increasingly unacceptable, no doubt. But in a word, no, I can't see it would cause me any grief or anxiety, whatever she wrote or didn't write about me. And pretty certainly she wouldn't have. Not important enough in her stellar career.'

'What about someone really important?'

'Hey hey, hold on. You don't have to rub it in. One tries not to dwell on one's insignificance.'

'You know what I mean.'

'Sadly I do. All too well. But I don't know the answer. Not being an important figure I don't know how an important figure might react.'

'Same here,' Plant said, attempting mollification. Not a word much used any more.

Chapter Ten

The phone rang.

'Mr Plant?'

'Yes. Who's that?'

'Sasha.'

She somehow made it sound like they were in a Cold War spy novel.

'The girl from the library,' she added when he didn't respond. 'You gave me your card.'

'The girl from the library,' Plant repeated.

'Sasha. Are there so many?'

'No, not at all,' Plant said. 'Not really, no,' he added.

'You wanted to meet my aunt.'

Did he? He didn't quite remember it like that.

'She's an old friend of Liz Lambastier's.'

'Oh yes.'

'So, do you want to meet her?'

Why not?

'Why not?' he said.

'Up to you.'

'When's convenient?' he asked.

Plant was not one of those who made a point of never crossing the Harbour Bridge when he was in Sydney. There were denizens of the inner west who saw the north shore as alien territory and never entered it. And vice versa. More and more Plant was finding all of it pretty alien. It didn't make much difference where he was. Even the familiar places were changing, had changed.

The upper north shore was not somewhere he had any familiarity with. Big, dark, red-brick houses, two storeys, small windows, high trees overarching the houses and roads and occasionally dropping branches through the roofs. It was all very shaded and gloomy, not the sun sparkling on the water vision of Sydney that he preferred. No need to go into the water, just enjoy looking at it. But up here it was another world. Cool beneath the trees, quiet, even the lawnmowers and leafblowers were at rest. All very old and silent and to Plant's susceptibilities menacing rather than peaceful. Dark, dark, dark amidst the blaze of noon.

He parked the car, walked up the driveway, pressed the doorbell, and the girl from the library greeted him.

'Oh, hello,' he said. 'I didn't realize you would be here.'

'Good morning to you, too,' Sasha said. 'Sorry about that.'

'No, it's no problem.'

'I didn't think it would be,' she said.

'No, it isn't, not at all.'

She looked at him with one of those I can see right through you looks.

'Come in,' she said, 'and meet my aunt.'

The aunt was a well-preserved, petite, sixty-something-year-old. Very well-preserved. Hair suggesting platinum though maybe closer to aluminium tints. But a sheen. And grooming. And wrapped loosely in colourful folds of fabric, lace, cotton, or for all he could tell without having to look more closely than seemed seemly, polyester. Hemp, could it even be hemp? She had a copy of Lambastier's *What I Did* on a round, glass table, a scattering of magazines beside it, the more upmarket ones, *Vogue*, *Gourmet Traveller*.

'This is Mr Plant, Aunt,' Sasha said, stressing the rhyme and smiling at it.

'Hilly Fann,' the aunt said.

The dedicatee of *What I Did*. Could it be? Had he heard correctly? When he had noted the dedication it had seemed more than a bit dubious, some sort of suggestive joke. He had assumed it was just one more fiction, not a real person at all. Yet here she was, smiling at him.

Hilly Fann's story was that they were at school together, she and Liz. Until Liz got expelled, that is, but they carried on being best friends even after that. In their mid-teens.

'I just tagged along,' she said. 'Most of the time I was terrified. She'd want to hang out at that pub in Balmain, the Forth and Clyde. I'd never been anywhere like it. Bikies and poets and mad people. Not that you could tell them apart. I was terrified of all those people. It was so crowded. And loud. This was when she was going to be a poet.

'I remember when she read her poems. It was a shambles. All these people getting wiped out down on the waterfront of this old, run-down garden. One of those big old sea captains' houses or whatever they were. Everyone called them sea captains' houses. They were all pretty much in ruins or carved up into rented rooms, no one wanted to live there in those days, except the poets who went anywhere where it was cheap. And it was cheap.

'I'd thought a poetry reading would be all, you know, artistic, sensitive. I used to sit in the school library all day reading poetry, Keats and stuff, Tennyson, that sort of thing. Knights and fair ladies and romance and beauty. And there was this drunken rabble drinking out of beer cans and sharing joints and shouting out if they didn't like what was read. They threw a bucket of water over one poet, off the top of the cliff down to where he was reading below. He just kept on reading. I was terrified for her.'

'And what happened to her?'

'Nothing. Nothing that I can remember. She just read.'

'No one threw a bucket of water over her or hit her with a beer can?'

'No.'

'They just listened?'

'I suppose so. I can't remember. Funny, you can remember the fear, but not what happened.'

'So she started out as a poet.'

'Yes.'

'Before she moved to travel writing.'

'Well, there's not a lot of money in poetry. I think she figured that out pretty soon. But she always liked to think of herself as a poet. Basically. Even if she had to write other things to survive.'

'She hung out with other poets?'

'For a while. Till they all fell out. Quarrelsome bunch. I thought they were awful. Dreadful, dishonest people.'

'What did they quarrel about?'

'Everything. Anything. They were like chooks in a chook pen. Pecking at each others' feathers for dominance. As if anyone was watching or cared. There was this huge, big fight over a poetry magazine. Can you imagine it? Of all the problems in the world. War. Starvation. Poverty. Nuclear weapons. And the only thing they get steamed up about is getting control of a pissy little poetry magazine. I mean, really.'

'And she was mixed up in that?'

'Up to her eyeballs. She loved it. All these stupid committee meetings and votes and expulsions and dissents from the chair. Ridiculous.'

'What happened?'

'I don't think anything happened. I mean one bunch of poets and their mates got control and wouldn't publish the other bunch.'

'Which bunch was she?'

'With the winners, naturally. Didn't I make that clear? She always managed to back the winning side. She was brilliant like that. Always seemed to know who was going to come out on top.'

'And she always did? Come out on top?'

'As far as I know. She was quite amazing, really. Quite a powerful figure, you might say.'

'Did she show you her poems?'

'Did she show me her poems? Really? What do you think?'

Sasha laughed.

'She was a poet,' Hilly said. 'That's what they do. Show you their poems. All day long and every day. Haven't you ever met any poets?'

'And you resented this?'

'Why would I resent it?'

'You sounded a bit...'

'Loud,' Sasha said. 'She always gets loud when she gets excited. Carried away.'

'I do not get carried away.'

'But it's all enthusiasm, not rage. Even if it sounds like rage.'

'I do not rage.'

'No, of course you don't.'

'What were they like?' Plant asked.

'What were what like?'

'The poems. Were they any good?'

'They were, actually.'

'What about her other writings. Did she show you them too?'

'Sure. Bits and pieces. When she was in town. Or she'd mail me something once in a while.'

'Published?'

'Yes. Clippings, usually. Sometimes a photocopy, maybe.'

'What about unpublished stuff?'

'What about it?'

'Did she show you that?'

'I suppose sometimes it would be something she'd just been writing so it mightn't have been published.'

'Did you keep it?'

'Keep what?'

'Any of the pieces that she sent you.'

'Oh, I might have. But not religiously. I didn't make a special collection, if that's what you mean.'

'What he means,' Sasha said, 'is do you have any unpublished writings of Liz's?'

'Oh, is that what he means? So why doesn't he say it?'

'He's getting round to it.'

'Why does he want to know that?'

'Because he's looking for some unpublished manuscript of Liz's.'

'Is he? Oh well, why would I know anything about that?'

'So you don't have anything?' Plant asked.

'Why would I?'

'She didn't leave anything with you?'

'Me? Why would she?'

He decided to come clean about what he was looking for. He couldn't see any obvious reason not to. Not now Sasha had managed to spell out his interest. He might have kept quiet about it, depending on what Hilly looked likely to come up with, but that option had gone now.

'There's supposed to be some last book she never published but no one knows where the manuscript is.'

'I'm sure I don't know,' Hilly said.

Plant didn't necessarily believe her. But there wasn't a lot he could do about it. There wasn't anything he could do about it as far as he could see.

'Would it be worth anything?' she asked.

'Probably not. Not a lot, anyway.'

'So why bother about it?'

'Her sister's interested in finding it. Maybe you could let me know if you hear anything.'

'Why would I hear anything?'

Plant could think of no good reason. He smiled, as far as he could in the circumstances.

'Why don't you make us a pot of tea, Sasha dear,' Hilly suggested. Sasha hopped up and headed for the kitchen. Hilly gestured at the copy of *What I Did* on the table beside her.

'Have you read it?' she asked.

He nodded.

'Enjoy it?'

'Yes, certainly.'

'What did you think of it?'

'Like the blurb described it, raunchy.'

'And how would you describe it?'

'Raunchy, I guess.'

She picked the book up and looked at it, shaking her head slowly from side to side.

'Wouldn't you agree?' he asked.

'I don't know,' she said. 'It's pretty much how it was.'

'What do you mean?'

'What I mean is, that was what it was like. That was the life we lived. A bit tarted up, maybe. And a bit sanitized. Well, a lot sanitized. But otherwise, yes, raunchy.'

'So it wasn't fiction?'

She giggled.

'Believe what you want,' she said. 'But the truth is, Liz didn't have much of an imagination. Why do you think she gave up writing fiction and turned to travel? She didn't know how to make it up. She didn't have any need to, luckily. She just put down what happened. Pretty much. She wasn't the imaginative type.'

Sasha returned with a tray and teapot and milk and sugar and three cups.

'Biscuits! Where are the biscuits, girl? We're not on a diet.'

Sasha pulled a face and disappeared in search of biscuits.

'I'm not putting her down. Not much, anyway. I mean, she came up with amazing ideas. And she did them. And then she wrote them down. Pretty much like it was. Could've been embarrassing, having a book like that dedicated to you. I freaked. I really did. Because she hadn't told me. First I knew was when she gave me a copy. Can you imagine?'

She put the book down and poured out the tea.

'But no one noticed. No one ever said anything. No one ever read the dedication page. Never even read the book, probably. So much for celebrity. Or if they did they thought it was just some name she'd made up. So they didn't think it was real. Any more than they'd think the book was. Still, she had it there under her belt, as it were. A bit lower down, maybe. The start of her brilliant career.'

She turned to Plant, a surge and swirl of soft summer fabric.

'And you've read it?'

'I only had time to skim, really.'

'Did you read the story about the media magnate?'

'The rich guy?'

'The rich guy who liked having dinner parties with a couple or more semi-naked chicks at the table while he fired his revolver at the chandelier. In between snorting cocaine and smoking weed and dropping speed, you name it, he had it.' She smiled. 'And we had it, wow, did we ever?'

'Was that...?'

Real, he would have asked, but she beat him to it.

'That wasn't half of it. She had to cut some of the stuff out, stuff he made us do. Disgusting.' She giggled. 'Ah my,' she said, reflectively, 'what we got up to. He was a complete full-on psycho. Pathetic. He used to hold us up by the ankles and get us to walk on our hands. Wheelbarrows, he called it. Make us walk on our hands to the end of the room and then he'd bang away.' She giggled some more. 'Makes me feel quite randy remembering it. Pathetic. What those poor guys had to do to get their rocks off.'

'Wasn't she taking a risk? What if he'd recognized himself and sued?'

'And make it all public? No. As it was, hardly anyone read the book and of those who did most would have assumed it was fiction.'

'Did he react?'

'No idea. He probably never read it.'

'He still might have heard about it. There might have been payback.'

'Could be. Not that I ever heard, though. Could be he was flattered. Like the Mafia love the way they get portrayed by Hollywood. He could've thought it was great. He could've called her up and asked her round and showered her with diamonds. After he'd screwed her a few times. He made her a columnist on his magazine, anyway. Or somebody did. Gave a new meaning to the word.'

'But he didn't try to stop publication.'

'Not that I heard. No, it came and went. There was a book launch, we all got wasted, and that was it. Maybe she got a grant on the strength of it. People started to know who she was. But that wasn't based on sales or anything. They were pathetic. She went overseas, anyway.'

'Where?'

'America, Asia, usual places. She'd look me up when she was back here. But basically we lost contact for years. I kept banging away, as it were, and she became a celebrity. Interviewed famous people. Travelled to famous places. From a feminist perspective, of course. She knew which side her bread was buttered.'

'You didn't really like her?'

'I liked her all right. She wasn't someone you admired especially. She was fun to be with. When she wasn't bad news. But she wasn't someone you ever got close to. At least I didn't. No, I just found her fun. Glad she became a celebrity, if that's what she wanted. Good for her. Why should I be envious?'

'No reason,' Plant said.

'Don't be ridiculous, there's every reason, of course I'm envious.'

She laughed.

'But what's a poor girl to do?'

'Have a chocolate biscuit,' Sasha suggested, 'what else?'

Hilly helped herself to a couple.

'Did she write any more about this stuff?' Plant asked. He reached across to the table and touched the book, just lightly, like he imagined the religious touched saintly relics. 'I mean, is there any more that she didn't put in *What I Did*?'

'There was a fair bit left out. She just wrote and wrote it, without any much planning, just getting stoned and hammering away there and belting out whatever challenging, outrageous, sexy, liberated, pornographic episode she could remember. And there were lots, let me tell you. And then she'd sit and sift through it all and pick out the bits she liked the best or that worked the best, basically.'

'So what did she leave out?'

'Bits that didn't work as a story. You've looked at it, it's just a series of episodes, the ones that weren't as crisp or pointed or poignant or whatever were left out. Doesn't mean they weren't true pictures.'

'So what happened to the material she didn't use?'

'No idea. Stashed away with her papers, I imagine. Whoever got them, her sister, maybe.'

'Her sister doesn't have them.'

'Ah well, her agent maybe. I don't know. There were some good stories she didn't use. Too true, some of them.'

'Like what?' Sasha asked.

'Oh, like we were having trouble with this bloke. Blokey sort of bloke. And this rich guy's driver...'

'The media magnate?'

'Yes, he had this dodgy ex-bouncer as a driver, like a bodyguard, anyway, his driver said to us one time he was taking us home, "That trouble you've got with that bloke," he said, "I can get it fixed for you. Five grand max." Which was kind of him, you know, offering to arrange a favour. Cheap at the price. And kneecapping only a hundred bucks. If we'd been less soft-hearted and all that, we might have been tempted to take him up on it.'

'But you didn't.'

'Really! What do you think?'

Plant didn't know what to think, preferred not to think about it at all.

'No, not me,' she said. 'I'm a vegetarian, I don't even kill animals. Why would I agree to something like that?'

'Why indeed?'

She gave him another hard look and laughed. Plant tried joining in, an uneasy chuckle. It was the best he could do.

'I used to be terrified of the things she got up to.'

'Fascinated, more like,' Sasha said.

'Appalled.'

'But always on hand for the next atrocity. True? True or false?'

'True or false,' Hilly agreed.

Chapter Eleven

'I've got something for you,' Fullalove said, sitting there rolling a joint and listening to a Willie Nelson album when Plant called in.

'What's that?' Plant asked.

'What you were looking for. Lambastier.'

'What, her missing manuscript?'

'Give it a go, mate. One of her travel books.'

'Oh,' Plant said.

'Gratitude, that's what I like about you, Plant. The way you express gratitude. Anyone else would have been thrilled.'

'I'm thrilled.'

'But really thrilled.'

'I'm as thrilled as I can be short of finding the manuscript. What is it you've got?'

'Like I said, one of her books of travel essays. *Tossed Overboard*. Actually, it's not bad. I might hang on to it. Give it back when you've looked at it. I might have misjudged her. A bit.'

'So now she's passed your suggestive filth and ideological purity test?'

'She's good on the live animal trade. Shipping sheep and cattle and goats from Australia to Asia and the Middle East. It's an appalling business. Hideous conditions.'

'I know,' Plant said, knowing quite enough about it, not wanting to know more. But Fullalove was remorseless.

'Thousands of them die, they're so cramped and overcome with heat. Literally. Twenty-four hundred they tossed overboard from one ship. Forty-three thousand sheep have died on board ships in the last five years. That's averaging nearly nine thousand a year. And that's just sheep. The figures...'

'I know, I know,' Plant tried again, louder this time, cutting him off, not that he knew the figures, but he would rather not know any more right now.

'Anyway,' Fullalove said cheerfully, unfazed, 'Lambastier exposed it years ago. Not that it's done any good, the horror still goes on.'

He handed the book over.

'It's just the one essay. But give it back to me. It's the sort of thing that might be hard to get, the way they kill stories like that. The meat-trade companies probably buy up any copies they can lay their hands on and destroy them. I might be able to get a good price for it.'

'Really?'

'Dunno. Worth a try, though. I bet your mate Mac Arber is onto it.'

'He only had her stories.'

'Of course. Did he say he'd look out for this one?'

'No.'

'There you are then. He's got a standing order for any copy that turns up.'

'Is that so?'

'Could be. You've got to consider it. Why not?'

Plant gave the book a cursory look.

'Thanks,' he said. 'But I can't bear to read about it. It's so atrocious.'

'Just close your eyes to it like the rest of the population.'

'I already know about it. But right now it's the manuscript I need to find.'

'Sure,' said Fullalove. 'Have you checked with her agent? Obvious place. She's probably got it locked away in her cabinet of forgotten works.'

'Is that likely?'

'It's what agents do,' Fullalove claimed. 'Lose stuff. Filter out anything too radical, too controversial. Send it to publishers who they know aren't going to take it. Or just file it with the forgotten.'

'Is that what they do?'

'Either by incompetence or design. Sure.'

'So if Lambastier's last manuscript was controversial...'

'A big if. But sure. Her agent could've sat on it. Or it could be jealousy. Competitiveness. I mean, wouldn't you?'

'Wouldn't I what?'

'Be tempted. If one of your authors was getting all this celebrity attention and partying with the A-list and you're slaving away reading shit seven days and nights a week, wouldn't you feel like, accidentally of course, just shafting said author? Sending the manuscript places it'll get rejected and then just filing it. Away somewhere.'

'You really think that could be the case?'

'It could be. Though not necessarily so in this case. But I wouldn't rule it out. Why don't you call in on Agent Orange and have a nose around her drawers?'

'I never know whether you deliberately aim at being distasteful or you just can't help it.'

'Puzzles me too,' Fullalove said.

'How do you know who her agent was?'

'I looked her up in a *Who's Who*.'

'She's dead. She wouldn't be in *Who's Who*.'

'That's why I keep the old volumes. Libraries throw them out. Which is a mistake. They're an invaluable resource.'

'If you want to live in the past.'

'You can't live in the future. Or the present, because as soon as it's present it's already passing.'

Plant sidestepped any further philosophical speculations from Fullalove.

'Agent Orange,' he said. It was enough just to say it, it filled him with foreboding.

'Who else? Money and power from a feminist perspective. She'll market men if there's money in it. But she loves telling men she can't sell their books. Which is neat, really. It means she doesn't get upset at publishers' rejections, which is good for business. No good being upset all the time and that's what publishers specialize in, rejecting things. So if it's some bloke's book she wallows in the enjoyment of telling him it's fucked, no one wants it. And having this feminist image she promotes women even if she resents them. No sisterly solidarity, just official PC feminism. Can't imagine she'd have really got along with Lambastier. Too similar. Two aggressive, ambitious, narcissistic sociopaths in the same line of business. Bet you she's got something in the files.'

'But would it be the unpublished manuscript? Why wouldn't she have sold it somewhere? Lambastier was marketable.'

'Depends what's in it. And when Lambastier gave it to her, how long before she died. With Lambastier dead she could just have buried it. Or cremated it. Or on the other hand kept it in the safe. Like the newspapers always keep the best stories in the safe and never publish them.

'Over the years she's developed a handful of star writers who were released from obscurity and foisted onto the vulnerable public. She would have worked on their manuscripts with them, suggesting leaving bits out if they were defamatory or self-incriminating. And the bits that were left out would've ended up in her cabinet of curiosities. Political scuttlebutt, gossip, leverage for blackmail or pressure or influence.'

'You know this?'

'Without a doubt.'

'So now you're saying I should be looking for off-cuts from her earlier books, not a missing manuscript.'

It fitted in with what Hilly Fann had told him about bits being cut out of that first story collection.

'Why assume the manuscript and the off-cuts are separate entities? What if they're the same?' Fullalove asked.

'They can't be.'

'Yes they can. The earlier material could have been incorporated. Expanded. Continued. Which would be a good reason to suppress it, if it contained dodgy stuff they'd had to cut out from earlier books.'

Plant phoned Agent Orange with some reluctance. There was a certain predictable sameness about literary agents in his experience. And he had had some experience. They tended to be women of a certain terrifying type. No doubt agents needed to be tough. So did private investigators. Research assistants and investigative reporters. But compared to the agents he encountered, he barely rated. Didn't rate, to be honest. No contest. And he hated getting into things he was predestined to be defeated in. Though what could an agent do to him? Refuse to read anything he might have written. Those days were gone, anyway. Pretty much. For the time being. But that fear of rejection still held its power. And rejection was the weapon always available to an agent. Of your entire personality, not just your manuscript.

He decided on the direct approach.

'Liz Lambastier. You were her agent.'

'I still am. In terms of her literary estate.'

'Good. Great.' He stopped himself from saying perfect but probably let slip a marvellous.

'I have been asked to locate some papers of Ms Lambastier's by her sister. I wondered if you might happen to have any. Or know where I might find them. Maybe we could meet...'

'Not a hope. I'm flat out. I can give you three minutes now.'

Not even five minutes. How could people be so busy? It made him simultaneously envious and appalled, unwanted and relieved.

'I'm trying to track down an unpublished manuscript of hers.'

'Well I don't have it.'

'I wondered if you might have any clues as to where it might be.'

'What was it about?'

'I don't know.'

'Travel?'

'No idea.'

'Animals? She got into animal welfare. When you can't get any more publicity for yourself, get into animals. Whales. Elephants. Live sheep trade. Take your pick.'

'I don't think so.'

'Anything else you don't know?'

'I don't even know if it exists.'

Agent Orange snorted contemptuously.

'So why are you calling me?'

'I thought maybe you might be holding papers of hers in your files.'

She snorted some more and added in some offensive words for good measure. Deeply offensive. And not short measure, she could not be accused of that, not in this context at least. That done, she returned to the chase.

'Papers? What do you mean papers?'

'Manuscripts.'

'Manuscripts?'

'Or typescripts. I don't know which, they could be either. Or printouts.'

'What sort of thing?'

'Well, an unpublished book. Or passages she cut out of her published books.'

'You looking for defamation?'

'No, not at all. Cuts made for length, maybe. I understand her first book...'

'No you don't. Nobody could understand what I went through with that. Cuts? Like a barber's shop, bits trimmed off everywhere. All over the floor. Literally. What a drama queen she was.'

'What happened to the bits that were cut out? Would she have thrown them out or kept them?'

'Liz? She was as mean as pig-shit. She never threw anything out. Except men.'

She gave a deep, satisfied laugh.

'No, she'd keep it all and re-use it. Make another book out of it. Or use it as the basis of one. You know, you can feel better if you can say, wow, now I've just got started and I've already got ten thousand words on file. A great morale lifter for fucked writers. Saves them from the abyss of the blank screen.'

'So would you happen to have any of that sort of material? Or some unpublished text?'

'You think if I had an unpublished work of Liz's I'd just let it lie around.'

'I don't know. Maybe waiting for the best time to publish it.'

'That gets further away every day.'

'So you don't have a box of...?'

'No, I don't have a manuscript or a typescript or any other fucking sort of script of hers or anybody else's, published or unpublished, I do not allow them in the fucking office. This is a paper-free fucking office, Plant, so manuscripts and typescripts are not welcome.'

'What about books?'

'Same deal. Paper-free, get it? That means excluded, get it? So no, I don't have any waste paper of hers lying around.'

But the possibility that there might be an unpublished, saleable book of Lambastier's lying around, however remote, had fired her interest. The possibility of a profitable sale muted her usual aggressiveness and calculated offensiveness. She still had the grating voice but at least she wasn't shouting.

'Though come to think of it, I think I might have a box of her back-up discs. Old floppies. Flash drives. She got me to store them in case anything happened to her computer on her travels. I never bothered to look at them. Maybe I should've. Shit. How am I going to read old floppy discs?'

'It has to be possible.'

'Of course it has to be possible. But how? Malicious little vixen, that's just the sort of evil stunt she'd pull, deposit a fucking book with me without telling me.'

'If you find the back-ups, could you let me know if anything looks like it might be what we're looking for?'

'How am I going to know what you're looking for?'

'If she labelled them...'

'Why would you believe the labels?'

An agent through and through. Never judge a book by its cover. Though Plant often did.

'Right. Gotta go,' she said. No polite courtesies of farewell, *auf wiedersehn, au revoir*. Just end of conversation.

Chapter Twelve

If Liz Lambastier had left a box of back-ups with her agent for safekeeping, the sooner they were safely in Plant's possession the better. Or copies of them. From his point of view, anyway. There were problems, of course. Agent Orange could very well be unwilling to release copies. But at least he could get her to check them out, surely, see that there was no obvious unpublished missing book amongst them. Just back-ups of published material. It was worth a try. Worth just turning up, without any advance warning. He set out first thing in the morning, off to the terrace in Glebe where Agent Orange had her office, an elegantly gentrified setting for her raucous negotiations. It sat behind what once had been a narrow patch of garden, now covered with white and grey pebbles, little chips of rock and stone, nothing living or growing amidst them at all. The iron railings fronting the street were painted a glowing gold. Agent Orange traded as Jacqueline Gold, which was no doubt her name, but everyone referred to her as Agent Orange.

'Plant, you fucker,' she greeted him, incandescent.

He'd had worse. Often enough. Nonetheless he was a little surprised at the force of it, still standing outside on the path, the torrent of words bombarding him like she'd got hold of a police Taser.

'I knew I shouldn't have taken your call. You're just bad news, Plant. Why don't I follow my instincts? I knew you were trouble as soon as it rang. I get a call from you and next thing I know I'm burgled.'

'Burgled?' Plant said. He wondered about saying he was sorry, even terribly sorry, but that could have been interpreted as a confession of complicity. He could feel the accusations shooting through the air like a flurry of poisoned darts.

'Yes, burgled. What a coincidence. You phone up asking if I've got some fucking manuscript and then amazingly it disappears overnight. Amazing, don't you think?'

'Amazing,' he agreed. 'So you did have it?'

'So just give them back.'

'Give what back?'

'The flash drives and floppy discs you stole.'

'I didn't steal anything.'

'Or got one of your low-life friends to steal.'

'Nothing to do with me,' he said.

'Why don't I believe you?'

'I don't know. But you should.'

He moved on the path there as if to suggest maybe they might continue this inside, but she stood blocking the doorway.

'Don't you tell me what I should or shouldn't do.'

'Sorry.'

'Don't even speak.'

He didn't even speak.

'What are you doing round here anyway? Lured back to the scene of the crime? Couldn't stay away?'

He tried shaking his head.

'What?' she demanded. 'Answer me.'

'I came to have a look at the back-ups.'

She laughed. The cackle of derision she had perfected for dealing with publishers' offers.

'I'm sure. You can tell that to the police.'

'I didn't take them,' he said. 'Really.'

'Cross your heart and hope to die,' she said, with a well-practised sneer.

'Sure,' he offered.

He began to make the sign of the cross. She made a snorting noise. Picked up in her horse-riding adolescence, no doubt.

'Have they all gone?' he asked.

'All what?'

'The back-ups.'

'What do you think? They sat there making a selection? "Oh, that's a pretty colour, let's take that one." "No, don't like the look of that old floppy, leave that."'

'So they've all gone.'

'Yes, you fucker.'

'Had you had a chance to look through them?'

'Why would I have done that?'

'After I called. Asking if there was an unpublished Lambastier manuscript.'

'And you think I've got nothing better to do than to run your filthy errands for you?'

'No, not at all. That's why I came round.'

'Why?'

'To have a look for myself.'

She glared at him.

'You have a fucking nerve,' she said.

He was glad to hear that. Always afraid he might be losing it. Confronted by people like her.

'No,' she said, 'I hadn't looked through them.'

'So you've no idea what was there.'

'Obviously not.'

'So you don't know if this missing work of Lambastier's was there.'

'No.'

'Ah well.'

'But I do know that it looks totally suspicious that you phone me up asking me if I have it and when I say I might I promptly get burgled.'

'Totally,' Plant agreed.

'And my suspicions are focused on you.'

'Oh now, come on,' Plant said, 'I didn't have anything to do with it.'

'You just set it in motion with your fucking phone call. Like detonating a fucking remote fucking bomb.'

'Maybe your phone's bugged,' he said.

'Why would my phone be bugged?'

Plant shrugged.

'Why not yours?'

He shrugged some more.

'Could I just have a look...?' he suggested, scene of the crime and all that.

'No you cannot have a fucking look. You can just fuck off. Now. Fuck off.'

She stood in her doorway, glowing like a thousand suns.

'Let me know if they turn up,' he said, retreating to the street. 'The floppies and flash drives.'

He didn't imagine they would. But it was worth suggesting to see the annoyance it generated in her, always splendid to watch once you were safely leaving.

Of course it might not have been a matter of phone bugging. Just of someone knowing that Plant was in pursuit of the missing work, and making the obvious deductions of where he would look. It was unlikely that Fullalove would have said anything. Unlikely that his conversations with Fullalove were overheard, unless the streets and cafes of Newtown were all bugged. Maybe they were. There might, of course, have been no connection between the robbery and the missing work of Lambastier's. Though unlikely. That Lambastier's agent was burgled at the time that Plant was looking for her missing manuscript, or allegedly missing manuscript, was too striking to be mere random coincidence. And though Fullalove was capable of being tight-lipped, Plant knew that the same could not be said of Mac Arber or Dennis or, for all he knew, of Hilly Fann and her niece. They all knew what he was looking for, might well have mentioned it casually, and the agent's was an obvious place to look. The information could have leaked out easily enough. It didn't necessarily require the assumption of a phone bug, and the implications that that immediately brought into play. Not necessarily.

Chapter Thirteen

Plant sat in his eyrie with a morning cup of tea. He surveyed the view of the city for a while, diverted himself with looking for signs of disaster, columns of smoke or helicopters hovering over crime scenes, but it all appeared calm and peaceful. Though appearances could be deceptive, probably were. He checked out the Lambastier travel book that Fullalove had found for him. Never judge a book by its cover. Fair enough. Nonetheless he checked the back-cover blurb again and the names attached to the endorsements.

It took him a while track down Felix Hacker. Not in the phone book, typical for somebody in the media and communications business. But he called Fullalove who found a landline number listed in an old *Who's Who* entry, so presumably there had once been an intention to maintain a certain sort of contact with someone or other. Posterity, could it be? He braced himself to make a cold call and struck lucky. Felix Hacker picked up on the second ring. Ever the editor, beside the hotline, even in redundancy and retirement.

There were some people you assumed were so eminent and so busy and so on-call and so distinguished that you felt fearful of ringing them. Plant was often fearful. He also knew now that these assumptions were often misguided. The once eminent and active were lucky if they stayed that way. Often they were bored and under-occupied and resentful of relegation to the scrapheap and more than eager to be interviewed, consulted, contribute to the public record, get their story out there. They were even accommodating in arranging to talk, willing to venture out, meet you halfway.

Hacker suggested the Queen Victoria Building in the middle of town.

Upstairs on level one, the Old Vienna Coffee House.

'How shall I recognize you?' Plant asked.

'I'll have a newspaper.'

'What, folded under your right arm, or held in your left hand or...?'

'Just to have a newspaper in this day and age is to be distinctive enough,' Felix said, in tones of doom. Or maybe just gloom. Tones, though, resonant.

He was sitting there waiting when Plant arrived, reading his paper and making notes in a little leather-bound notebook with a Mont Blanc ballpoint pen, looking like a Middle European spy from a World War II movie, the crumpled suit jacket bunched up at his neck, the frayed shirt collar with the tip buckled, the bow tie, modest in size, not one of the big floppy ones, but still making some status assertion or claim, pretty much unavailingly. No Smoking regulations spoiled the historic authenticity of the scene. But it was a fair approximation. Hacker had taken a table beside the railing at the edge of the serving area. Plant peered over it at the floor below, like peering down into those nineteenth century French arcades once so beloved of cultural commentators, Felix the faded flâneur, the bereft boulevardier, washed up on some alien shore.

'Liz Lambastier,' Plant said, introductions dealt with. 'You wrote an endorsement for her book.'

'Did I?'

'It has your name to it.'

'That means nothing,' he said. There was a marked trace of Old Vienna in his accent. 'The publisher could have written it. She could have written it. She was pretty smart at things like that. Dictating words to put in your mouth. Makings of a good journalist. She was good, no doubt about it.'

'You knew her.'

'Of course I knew her. You've read my memoir.'

Plant was too slow, he faltered.

'You should,' Hacker assured him. 'You can get it across the road at Abbey's bookshop there. I would give you a copy except that it is one of my core beliefs that people should pay for books. If they believe in sustaining a cultural tradition.'

His voice was both guttural and yet melodic. Talking was one of its pleasures.

'And if we don't believe in that,' he asked, 'what is it that we do we believe in?'

'Fair enough,' said Plant.

'Those were the days,' Hacker said.

Plant nodded respectfully, encouragingly, though there was probably no need for either. Hacker was in full spate.

'When there were still the magazines. Forget newspapers, who cares about newspapers? They have their place, but it was the magazines that had the quality. Weekly, fortnightly, monthly. That's where you'd get considered opinion and informed commentary. A natural home for someone like her. Considered pieces, background briefings. Time to reflect. The trouble with newspapers is that you are always chasing the news. You have to keep running. The internet has got them licked for breaking news. But the weeklies...'

'And they were what Lambastier wrote for?' Plant asked, getting back on track, his track anyway.

'She came up to me at some function or other. I can't remember where. She must have staked me out. She came up to me and said, "I am going to be travelling through Asia and the Middle East. How about I send you some pieces?" Well, I mean, what is a chap to do?'

'I don't know.'

'You've got two minutes, you don't know this creature from Eve, she's caught you off guard, so what have you got to lose, if the copy's no good you don't have to run it, she'll be out of the country so she won't be charging into the office abusing you when it doesn't appear, so naturally, what should I do...?'

'And that's how her career began?' Plant asked. 'You gave her her big break?' he added, personalizing it, giving credit where credit was due, and where it was eagerly awaited.

Hacker beamed with the satisfaction of achieving a place in journalistic history. The man who discovered Liz Lambastier.

'And the copy she sent in, was it usable?'

'You've read it, haven't you?'

Had he? He should have done. But where would he have found old copies of the magazine?

'That was the material she collected in her book?' he tried.

'Yes.'

'The one you endorsed? *Tossed Overboard*?'

'Yes.'

'And you thought it was top quality?'

'Not just me.'

'But you were the editor. You published it first-off.'

Hacker couldn't help exuding self-satisfaction. Made no effort not to. He gave a silent, modest nod. And a couple more to make certain.

'Why was she going to Asia?'

'She wanted to travel, why else? They were all into travel back then. Still are. From hippy trail to gap year. It's all right when you're young. Too damn uncomfortable when you get older.'

'Did you keep in touch?'

'Oh yes. Naturally.'

'Regularly?'

'Once in a while.'

'But not more?'

'Why would she? Those days came to an end. She moved on. The magazine folded. All the magazines folded.'

'Really?' Plant said. More as a matter of punctuating the conversation than asking for substantiating information. But he got it. The information. Hacker embraced the opportunity to hold forth. Like in the old days on the phone to the copy-takers, dictating your deathless prose, before the time came when you had to do it all yourself, key it in and take your own photographs.

'Magazines,' Hacker was saying. 'They were my life. I lived and breathed them. From school onwards. School magazines, university magazines, I got bitten by the bug. So out in the big wide world, that's what I did. Magazines. I read them. I wrote for them. I edited them. I loved them.'

'And now they no longer exist.'

He glared at Plant as if Plant were somehow responsible for their demise.

'You know,' he said, 'I went down to my local shopping mall, not long ago, I went down to the newsagents. And it wasn't there. This huge shopping mall and no newsagent. The bookshop went years ago. Now the newsagent had gone. So, I find one down in the next suburb, I wander in, I buy the weekly I am looking for and you know what it said? This is the last print issue. From next week it's only available online.

'*Gott im Himmel.* It was like the end of an era. Well, it was the end of an era. The end of the world, in fact. My world. All finished. It's a past world now, that world of the magazines.'

'I guess it is,' Plant agreed, sitting there in the Old Vienna Coffee House in the Queen Victoria Building.

'Three hundred years of cultural history. All gone. I mean, really, the Nazis burn books and magazines and we fight a war to defeat them and what happens now? Now we burn our own magazines ourselves, we don't even burn them, there is nothing to burn, we simply stop publishing them. I ask you, what sort of victory is that?'

'Did she write a lot for you?'

'What's a lot?'

'Did she write regularly? Every issue?'

'Not every issue, no. But enough to make her name.'

'And it's all collected in the book you endorsed.'

'I shouldn't think so, no, not all of it.'

'So there could be another book.'

'She might have collected some of the pieces in another book, yes, you'd have to look.'

'But would there be enough pieces that she didn't collect for an unpublished book?'

'Possibly. I've never really thought about it.'

'But you don't know of one.'

'Why would I? No idea.'

'Her sister thought there was an unpublished manuscript.'

'Where?'

'That's the question. No one knows.'

'I can't help you there. What was it supposed to be about?'

'I don't know.'

'Well, if you don't know what it's about and you don't know where it is you might have a problem finding it, don't you think?

'Looks like it,' Plant agreed.

He followed Hacker's suggestion and went across the road into Abbey's bookshop. He felt more at home there than amongst the high-end tourist-market shops of the QVB. Too expensive. Not his world. He was happier amongst the fiction and biography and history of the bookstore. To say nothing of the lies and disinformation. But all waiting to be decoded. The raw materials of research waiting to be processed. He browsed along the memoirs and autobiographies and biographies, endless actors, singers, athletes, politicians. The occasional near literary experience. And Felix Hacker's record of a long and happy life. He flicked through the index. Lambastier, Liz, featured. A fair few references. More than he could decently transcribe standing there. He took it to the counter, flicking through the pages as he went. The title page had been scrawled on, smudgy black ink leaching through the cheap paper. Felix Hacker's signature, no less.

'This copy has been scribbled on,' he told the cashier. 'Any chance of a discount?'

She shook her head.

He walked past the statue of Queen Victoria, bought from Ireland within living memory, Plant's memory anyway though he couldn't remember the date, and past the busker beside it and on past the Town Hall and St Andrew's cathedral and then across George Street and along Bathurst Street and into Pitt Street and past the Edinburgh Castle where

Henry Lawson once lived and drank. Verses from his 'Faces in the Street' blown up poster-size and on display in the window. Nice touch. Respect for history and literature. Though they hadn't displayed the crucial lines:

The warning pen shall write in vain, the warning voice grow hoarse,
But not until a city feels Red Revolution's feet
Shall its sad people miss awhile the terrors of the street.

Maybe he could incite Fullalove to go down there one night and add the missing lines. Except that ever since the excuse of the Olympics the streets had been systematically saturated with surveillance cameras. Maybe leave it alone. He walked on past. Looking up from the cavern of the street above the old nineteenth-century facades, and up above the multiplying high-rise towers behind them that used all the force of Mammon to exclude the light, and yet failed, he could see the vivid blue of the cloudless sky. A perfect Sydney sky.

He gave one last look and headed down into the cool basement of the Greeks with his purchase. Something to read over a half carafe of retsina, bread and olive oil, vegetarian moussaka. 'Menus that time forgot' a sign in the doorway announced. And baklava, why not baklava once in a while, or even galatoboureko, why not? Something to sweeten Felix Hacker's celebration of a life well lived. Felix's life. And the famous people he had known. Including a few, fond memories of Liz. How he had spotted her, seen her talent, hired her, sent her overseas and launched her on the path to international celebrity.

Chapter Fourteen

Fullalove put on his baseball cap as they left his house. It did nothing for his appearance. Or did a lot but nothing positive in Plant's eyes. Given Fullalove's profound distaste for the American way of life and its foreign policy, it was a strange thing for him to wear. As unlikely as a bowler hat, insignia of that other evil empire for which Fullalove had similarly negative feelings. But a bowler hat might have been too distinctive for Fullalove's wish to live in the shadows, whereas baseball caps were common currency along King Street. Nonetheless Plant questioned him about it. The cap.

'Anti-surveillance,' Fullalove explained. 'All those cameras along the streets and in the shopping malls and outside the banks. The peak stops them picking up your face on camera and running their facial recognition software. Too hot for a hoodie, this weather.'

Plant envisaged him in a hoodie and shuddered. It was an image from a medieval dance of death, the grim reaper, the cowled, skeletal figure. It fitted all too well with other aspects of Fullalove's life, mad monkish librarian or market-trader scrap-merchant for old books. Maybe the baseball cap was preferable. Preferable to Plant, at least.

'Where did you get it?'

'Vinnies. Brilliant, innit?'

'Is it a collector's item?'

'No way. Don't be idiotic. Totally generic, middle of the road, mass market, made in China. Nothing distinct, nothing identifiable about it.'

'How can you bear wearing a second-hand cap? Second-head cap. All that sweat and dandruff. Psoriasis. You could get a new one for ten bucks.'

'You're phobic.'

'Sure am.'

'We all are,' Fullalove conceded. 'But in different areas. I'm phobic about security. I admit it. No problem. So I buy stuff for cash at charity shops. Then there's no serial number or batch number recorded that will trace it back to some supplier who might lead to the shop and the sales assistant who remembers you, me.'

'Why would that matter unless you're planning some major crime?'

'It matters in principle,' Fullalove said. 'You observe security procedures in every area. Never know when you could get set up or picked off. So on principle pay cash, go to charity shops...'

'For everything?'

'To save money for a kick-off. But no, not for everything. Can't do food.'

'A pity,' Plant said. Sarcastically.

'A serious pity,' Fullalove agreed. 'Someone gets to know your eating habits, that's how they can kill you, toxins injected into whatever they figure you'll buy this morning, listeria, botulism, nerve-agent, you name it, so what if it kills a dozen or so other people who buy the same product, makes it look random, like those shopping mall and nightclub shootings and the rest of the massacres, Oklahoma bombing, Port Arthur, Lockerbie, you never know whether there wasn't one specific target amongst it all and the rest collateral damage as they love to put it. So keep your food preferences secret. You don't want to end up biting into a poisoned apple.'

Plant was struck dumb. Dumbstruck. Speechless. Without words. The thesaurus entries sped before his eyes but nothing was uttered.

'So all you can do is avoid going to the same shop all the time. And don't buy the same things every time. Same with restaurants. Cafes. Pubs. Don't have a regular, observable routine. It's a maxim of a wise man never to return by the same road he came, providing another's free to him.'

'Is that so?'

'Walter Scott two centuries ago. *Rob Roy*.'

There seemed no point in saying anything. It all made sense. Even if it was unlikely and over the top. Excessive.

'Sure it's excessive,' Fullalove agreed. 'Sure it's all unlikely and improbable. But probability's just a matter of statistics. Of calculation. That half a percent chance could be the difference between life and death. You get identified in the wrong place at the wrong time, you've had it. So, first off, never get identified.'

He pulled the cap brim down lower over his forehead. All Plant could see was a satisfied grin, lips flecked with rolling tobacco, teeth stained.

'Doesn't going to different shops eventually increase the chance of your being monitored?' Plant asked. 'You end up going to half a dozen shops instead of just one, and out of six salespeople you've got a good chance one could be collaborating with the secret state. So instead of dealing with just one regular, bleary-eyed indifferent shopkeeper you spread yourself around and get nobbled.'

'It's a calculated risk. Like all of life.'

There seemed little point in saying anything to that. Just a roll of the eyes. After first closing them. Risk management.

'You should apply for one of those Health and Safety jobs, they'd love all this carry on.'

Fullalove shook his head. 'They've got other agendas beneath that Health and Safety bullshit.'

'Of course,' Plant said. 'How could I not have thought of that?'

'You need to be more paranoid.'

'Have you ever considered,' Plant said, 'that all your anti-surveillance tricks make you stick out like a prime suspect? No credit card, only cash transactions, no internet history, no social media profile, no obvious work hours, curtains drawn, never talk to neighbours, it's the classic profile of someone inviting being put under surveillance.'

'I'll take the risk,' Fullalove said. 'If it's true as they claim, which I doubt, that the security services don't conduct mass surveillance of people's phone and internet and banking and travel and credit card records, there is nothing, as far as I know, that prevents them from purchasing the data already acquired by commercial enterprises. It's all available on the open market. Why wouldn't they buy all that personal data that Facebook and Google and the rest of them harvest? All the likes, dislikes, beliefs, prejudices, friends, associates, internet searches, e-book purchases and so on. They wouldn't be doing their job if they didn't, would they? So why make it easy for them to get a fix on you?'

Fullalove was in fine form. Fine from Fullalove's perspective. Irritating and annoying to most other people. He sat there munching on an almond croissant, flakes of pastry flying around as he talked and gestured with it.

'How do you know she's dead?' he asked.

'Who?'

'Liz Lambastier.'

'Of course she's dead.'

'How do you know?'

'I don't know, read it in the papers probably.'

'Never believe what you read in the papers.'

'Oh, for heaven's sake.'

'It's an old saying but that doesn't diminish its truth.'

'Why wouldn't she be dead?'

'That, if I may say so, is a strange formulation. Maybe she preferred not to be. I'd check it out, anyway. She might've staged a disappearance, planning a comeback as someone else. Are you sure her sister really is her sister? Did she even have a sister? Is the sister maybe actually her pretending to be her sister?'

'That tired old plot.'

'Don't knock it, it's got fashionable again. Identity theft. A growth industry thanks to the internet.'

'Forget it,' Plant said. 'I've met her sister.'

'Sure. But do you know she actually is the sister? You may have met her, yes, but do you know the family?'

'No, I don't know the family.'

'Maybe you should check it out.'

'Forget it,' Plant said again. But the seed of doubt had been sown.

More than one seed. Maybe Lambastier was still alive. Maybe she'd been murdered. Maybe, maybe...

'So,' Fullalove said, 'she was a player in the takeover of a traditional, old-world-culture poetry magazine, and its transformation into postmodern imitation Americana. And she gets a regular spot in a so-called independent magazine reporting on her travels in Asia and the Middle East. So what do we deduce from that?'

'The literary life,' Plant suggested.

Fullalove gave his long, hard look. 'You know, there are still times when I can't work out whether you're just naive or dumb, or deliberately bloody obtuse. Reassure me, you're not an idiot by birth, just by provocative choice. It's some game you play.'

Plant gave his puzzled look. Mugging it just enough to give Fullalove further doubt as to is authenticity.

'Come on, what does that career path suggest?' Fullalove asked.

'You tell me. As I'm sure you're just dying to.'

'Who would be running a coup to take over a poetry magazine?'

'It's hard to imagine.'

'No it isn't. Not at all. Who was promoting Abstract Expressionism and postmodernism?' He didn't wait for a response. 'The Americans.'

'Surprise, surprise,' Plant said. 'Who else? Isn't it always them?'

'Pretty much.'

'And seizing control of a poetry magazine with a circulation of four or five hundred copies maximum would be high on their list of priorities.'

'Exactly.'

Plant laughed. Tried a laugh. But he knew he was going to be defeated.

'They did it with art, they obviously did it with literature.'

'Obviously,' Plant parroted, with a full, sceptical subtext.

'The CIA funded the big international tour of Abstract Expressionists.'

'I've already had Dennis banging on about that.'

'So,' said Fullalove. 'They needed to promote this empty, boring shit to kill off real art. Same with literature. Promote the American way of life, replace social content and human interest and moral value with empty formalism, that way you've fucked over your intelligentsia, castrated and sterilized your creative class, and cleared the way for the American Imperium.'

Plant drained the last of his English breakfast tea.

'I'm losing touch here,' he said, but he wasn't, he had heard it all before from Dennis. 'Are you saying the takeover of this poetry magazine was part of the grand strategy of American foreign policy? Am I hearing you correctly?'

'You control the intelligentsia, you've got control. The entertainment market is already controlled, crap films from Hollywood, crap television. Tidy up the creative end of things and you've got control of everything then.'

'And by tidy up you mean, what, kill...?'

'Take over. Suborn. Buy. Bribe. Steal. Easy enough. What would you do for a regular space in a magazine, Plant? Your own column. How much to buy your complicity? What wouldn't you do to secure that?'

'No one's offered it to me.'

'But they offered it to Lambastier, didn't they?'

'She certainly seemed to get it,' Plant agreed.

'And we know how these things are done, don't we?'

'Tell me. Talent, merit?'

'Patronage. Someone spots you.'

'Not in my case,' Plant said.

'We're not dealing with your case.'

'I thought you were asking what I would do for a regular by-line.'

'That was by way of example. I'm asking, what does this suggest about Lambastier?'

'You'll have to tell me.'

'It puts a different perspective on her. She was connected. She was on the payroll.'

'We don't know that.'

'Yes we do. Contextually. She has to have been. Somewhere along the line she got recruited. At university. Round the literary scene. Maybe at school, even.'

'I make that three times she was recruited.'

'Could be.'

'That's absurd. How could it be?'

'Why not? There are spotters out there all over the place. No reason why only one person would see her potential. Doesn't mean she was getting three salaries. Though there again, it's a thought, why not?' He shook his head reflectively. Three salaries. Tax free.

'So?'

'So. This isn't just about a missing manuscript. This is something else again.'

Plant sat there silent. Of course it was something else again. How could he ever have imagined it was something simple and straightforward? Just a library search. As if a library search wasn't bad enough. What he would have given for a regular well-paid spot on a magazine. Not that there were many magazines left. On the internet then. Or a paid blog. Or had the concept of being paid vanished now along with everything else?

'As far as I know I've just been asked to track down a manuscript.'

'Then you need to know more. Have you talked to Murray Brittan?'

'I don't think he'd be that easy to get through to.'

'Probably not. But he published the magazine that got her into the big time.'

'And he'd tell me if the CIA was paying her salary? Or his, for that matter?'

'What about Felix Hacker? Have you talked to him? He was the editor.'

'Sure. He said she told him she was going to be travelling through Asia so he agreed to her offer to send him stuff.'

'You think he took her on just like that?'

'Why not? She could write. She had a name.'

'Not then she didn't. The pieces she wrote for Hacker got her her name. That's where people first read her. Forget the poetry. No one read that. Or the stories. But giving her a regular spot in his magazine, that's what got her established.'

'You know this?'

'I used to read it. Before I got wise.'

'Got wise to what?'

'The magazine. That it was a fraud. Murray Brittan had this handful of magazines – two or three trade ones, a glossy women's mag under licence from the USA, a seedy tits and bums men's magazine, and then out of the blue he started this weekly. It was effectively a spoiler, to stop anyone setting up a serious magazine with some decent political commentary and analysis. This was just a distraction. Pseudo-alternative. All the chattering classes' fads. You know, that tired old new journalist number, all about the writer's feelings and failings and forgetfulness, look at me, me, me and forget the fucking subject, I am the subject. That sort of stuff. Not even stoned any more. Just fucking tedious. Same with the reviews, all about the reviewer. Useless if you wanted to know whether a movie or a play might be worth spending good money on. They scattered a few rude words through the text and ran some infantile facetious cartoons and thought they were being challenging and satirical. Well, the readers did. Who knows what the editor and publisher thought? Something a fair bit more calculating. Never seemed legitimate as a commercial proposition, anyway. You could do the figures. Not enough advertising to pay for it and not enough circulation to get enough advertising.'

'So why did he publish it?'

'Influence, obviously.'

'Influence?'

'The shadowy interface of politics and journalism. Exerting political pressure. Putting some up-and-coming politicians, or their wives, on his payroll and running their by-line once in a while. Pushing some line or other.'

'What line?'

'Whatever his backers required. From Thatcherism and Reaganomics to the war on terror to political correctness to same-sex marriage. Sometimes it might give two sides of an issue: but one side was always weaker. Use some incompetent leftie. There's lots of them around.'

'And that's what it was about?'

'Pretty much.'

'And Lambastier fitted in, you're saying.'

'Like a glove. Or a hand. Whichever. Feminist travelogue. The sufferings of Middle Eastern women. The triumph of Middle Eastern women. Animal rights. You know, mood pieces, scene setting, interviews with the significant. Then she glued it altogether and made a book out of it. Got a prize. Got another. You know, women's writing prize, travel-writing prize. Home and pantihosed.'

'And set for life,' Plant reflected. Not without a certain retrospective envy. 'Foreign correspondent on a roving assignment.'

'Hardly,' Fullalove said.

'Steady income. Cheap to live in Asia.'

'None of these magazines ever paid their way. So they didn't go around paying massive retainers and offering huge travel expenses.'

'So why was she doing it? How was she doing it?'

'You tell me.'

'Dope, I imagine. Isn't that why everyone went on the hippy trail?'

It was not something Plant had done himself. The hippy trail. He'd been to Asia. Got sick. Seen enough to decide that parasites and fevers and intestinal horrors and hepatitis A to Z outweighed the attractions of cheap drugs. He was protectionist on this. Buy Australian.

'Though I don't know,' Plant added, 'why would you do it to yourself? Why put yourself through it all? Just to get stoned.'

'She probably didn't.'

'What do you mean?'

'She probably had other reasons. Almost certainly did.'

'Like being a badly-paid stringer?'

'Provides a good cover.'

'Oh no,' Plant said.

Fullalove grinned. 'Oyez, oyez, oyez,' he intoned, flexing his wrist as if he were ringing a handbell.

'None of those magazines was ever real,' Fullalove said.

'What do you mean? They came out every week or every month. Isn't that real enough?'

'No,' Fullalove said, curt and certain.

'Go on, tell me.'

'They were never viable. None of them. Not enough advertising, not enough circulation. They all had to be subsidized, they never paid their way. So it's rich backers peddling influence. You can look at them worldwide. Sure, they had good journalism. Lively stuff you didn't get in the dailies. But basically they were all pushing a line.'

'The same line?'

'They all lost money so they were backed by people with money and basically people with money have the same line, wouldn't you say?'

'You tell me.'

'And half the time if not more, the people supposedly with money were just conduits for other people's money.'

'Go on.'

'Our money, in fact. Tax-payers' money.'

'You don't pay any tax.'

'Sure do. If you want to live outside of the law, you've got to be honest, as the man says.'

'Losing you here. How is it tax-payers' money?'

'Through government funds. Funnelled through secret service accounts, shonky foundations and institutes.'

'Start again,' Plant said.

'One, magazines of influence don't sell enough copies to pay their way. Two, they used to be subsidized by rich people with interests to protect and agendas to promote. Three, as the rich people ran out of money and the state became more intrusive, the magazines were propped up by secret government funds. Four, now most of them are defunct or dying and the funding's moved to the internet.'

'So forget the free press.'

'Exactly.'

'And you're saying the magazine she wrote for...'

'And made her name on.'

'And made her name on, was all the time subsidized by...'

'The usual suspects.'

'Did she know?'

Fullalove put on a look of unprejudiced inquiry.

'What about Felix Hacker? You think he knew?'

Fullalove sustained impassivity.

Plant reflected. The usual can of worms. What else did he expect from consulting with Fullalove? Why else had he consulted Fullalove? No surprises there. But what impact did it have on his research into Lambastier? Did it matter? Wasn't it a diversion best not pursued? Did it matter either way who paid the piper, wasn't the issue just to find out if there were any more tunes she'd piped that hadn't been played in public? But now that Fullalove had established a context, mightn't that be a bit tricky? If there was this other unpublished manuscript, might it contain material best left alone? Might that be why it was missing? Assuming it ever existed.

'So you're saying the magazine Hacker edited was funded by some government agency? Which?'

'What does it matter? Australian, American, British, Israeli or whatever, they're all in cahoots, doing each other's dirty work, could have been any of them.'

'So his hiring Lambastier to travel in Asia and the Middle East could have been giving her journalistic cover for agency work in the region. And his lack of interest in the missing manuscript may not be true, he may even as we speak be hot on the trail.'

Fullalove nodded agreement, uttering no further words that might be monitored or archived.

Chapter Fifteen

The one obvious person Plant hadn't approached yet was Murray Brittan. By checking out Lambastier's other contacts he had managed to postpone dealing with the media magnate. It had to be done. But media magnates were not the sort of people you could just drop in on. Or make an appointment with. He could delay the inevitable by doing a bit of research and investigation on Brittan's background. But that was only a delay. Nevertheless he did it. The research. Up to a point. Easiest was to check him out with Fullalove who'd had his moments in media, brief as they were and fewer as they had become.

'No, never worked for him,' Fullalove said.

'Why's that?'

'Just never happened. He was basically into buying people and I guess I never looked like a good buy.'

'Buying people? What do you mean? Like slaves?'

'Pretty much. Look at all the political figures who got their start with him. Great talent-spotter. Signed up these youngsters, put them on the payroll as journalists or lawyers, had them in his pocket ever after. Federal, state, nobbled them all. And their wives and girlfriends. And boyfriends. They'd all get their by-lines. How did he know they would all become so successful?'

'How?' Plant asked.

'The mysterious underpinnings of oligarchy beneath the peeling veneer of democracy.'

'Where did you read that?'

'I wrote it.'

'Where?'

'At my kitchen table.'

'I mean where did it appear?'

'It never did. Where do you think you could publish anything like that?'

'So it remains a missing, unpublished manuscript like Lambastier's.'

'Not missing,' Fullalove assured him. 'I can print you out a copy.'

'So how did he spot these people? Did he have a good research department? Or did someone else, and they called him up and tipped him off to find a slot for someone?'

Plant looked at Fullalove for an answer and Fullalove just looked back. Back at Plant and his question. There was nothing to say. The answer was both unknowable and obvious.

'And Lambastier was someone he spotted?'

Fullalove remained impassive.

'Or someone spotted her for him.'

Fullalove nodded.

'And he put her on the payroll.'

Another nod.

'And published her travel books.'

Another nod.

'So if this missing manuscript ever existed, she might have sent it to him, since he was her publisher.'

'Could be,' Fullalove agreed.

'So if anyone's got it, it would be him.'

'Might be.'

'Except he's never published it.'

'No.'

'So maybe it doesn't exist after all.'

'Maybe it wasn't any good.'

'Or maybe he suppressed it. Why didn't we think of this before?'

'Not my case,' Fullalove said.

Not really an adequate response in Plant's opinion. But there was no point in recrimination. No way he could convincingly blame anyone else. No way he could postpone the inevitable. He was going to have to talk to Murray Brittan.

'Tell me what you know about him,' Plant asked.

'There's a whole context here you need to look at.'

'I guess. If you say so.'

'You know it's true. You'd just rather talk to young chicks and old hookers. And you're missing the big picture.'

'Go on.'

'Brittan's magazine. It was like all of them. It was never viable. Either he ran it at a loss because of the influence it gave him, or it was a tax loss offsetting the obscene profits he was making elsewhere from the deals he was doing through the political contacts he'd nurtured. Or on top of that maybe it had a subsidy, like those old Cultural Freedom magazines.'

'You're saying it was CIA-funded.'

'Or one of the agencies. None of those magazines ever broke even. They were all propped up one way or another.'

'So how did Murray Brittan make his money? It wouldn't have been through publishing if his flagship magazine ran at a loss.'

'The thing about publishing, like any other business, is there are always opportunities for fiddling – so-called damaged stock, returns, how do you know they printed twenty thousand and had to pulp three quarters of them? It's not hard to arrange write-offs. Plus the old fire and flood trick at the warehouse. If you're into publishing you'd have more than one set of books. But who knows? Maybe he married money. Maybe he married debt which he acquired for tax write-offs.'

'Can you do that?'

'Probably.'

'You don't know.'

'If I knew the tricks of high finance would I be living like I do?'

'Unless it's your cover story to conceal great wealth.'

Fullalove grinned. Enigmatic in intention, uninviting in effect.

Plant sneezed. A couple of times, quite savagely. Then a racking cough.

'Pollen allergy,' he explained.

He sneezed again. He could see Fullalove flinching, positively withdrawing, retracting the hairs on his arms. He knew what Fullalove was thinking. Fullalove's world conspiracy views incorporated the world of virus manufacture. But this wasn't a virus. This was the wind-blown fertilization of the native flora. A seasonal sexual frenzy. 'Then blood shall stain the wattle,' as Henry Lawson wrote, envisaging revolutionary action. More likely from coughing up sputum.

'How can you have pollen allergy in the inner-city?' Fullalove asked.

'It's all the gentrification, everyone planting Australian natives.'

'It's more likely from being close to the university,' Fullalove said.

'What, from the trees in the grounds?'

'Forget the trees,' Fullalove said, darkly. 'The emanations of the mind prison.'

'Bad vibes?'

'Not just vibes.'

'Go on.'

'Toxic chemicals. Nerve agents. Mutant viruses escaped from some laboratory. Chemical warfare projects in development.'

'How come it doesn't affect you?'

'How do you know it doesn't?' Fullalove said. 'Or maybe I'm immune.'

He produced a distasteful looking rag from the pocket of his jeans and blew his nose.

'Check out Murray Brittan,' he said.

'How am I going to do that?'

'Make a phone call?'

'I doubt he'd take it.'

'Maybe not.'

'So what do I do?'

'Find someone who knows him.'

'I don't know anyone who knows him.'

'Have you given Luke a call?'

'Who's Luke?'

'Dealer to the stars.'

'What stars?'

'Those dead things lost in space whose light waves are still reaching us, all to no avail.'

'Fullalove, you have lost me too.'

'The expanding universe, all of us getting further and further away from each other. Do they still believe that?'

'Do who believe what?'

'Scientists and witch doctors. Or have they come up with another bright idea? They're like Trotskyites, scientists. Permanent revolution. Nothing is ever true. Everything endlessly overturned and superseded and replaced by something else that in its turn will be overturned.'

'What's this got to do with this Luke, whoever he is?'

'Not a lot,' Fullalove conceded.

'The stars,' Plant persisted.

'All those eager, ambitious movie-makers and novelists and political commentators and playwrights and actors who invaded the inner-city looking for sex and drugs. Some made it. Some didn't, still hanging in there, ghosts shuffling in through his doorway from the graveyard, begging for half an ounce, desperate ingratiating smiles, but you know the smile died aeons ago and there's nothing behind it except a black hole, the last flickering emissions giving an illusion of life.'

'You paint a very moving picture. And this Luke...?'

'He was their dealer of choice. Very selective. Only artistic souls supplied. No low-life around. The low-life was kept strictly below stairs.'

'Fullalove, I have no idea what you're talking about. What stairs? Are you stoned or something?'

'Taking the last question first, as politicians like to do, the answer is probably yes. Undoubtedly. As for the other issue, I spoke metaphorically. As I recall his was a house without stairs. All on the level, the only thing about him that was. As for what I'm talking about, his dealership was a sanitized one for bourgeois creative susceptibilities. No criminal element on show. No growers in the drawing room exuding the odours of liquid manure or blood and bone fertilizer.'

'So?'

'So it could be worth your while contacting him. Being a dealer is like being a media magnate. You get to know a lot about a lot of people. Gives you a lot of power potential. Murray Brittan and La Lambastier would have been on his circuit.'

'Is that a fact or a guess?'

'They all used to hang out together. When Murray first started he used to slum it a bit with the old political journalistic literary intelligentsia down at the pub.'

'Which pub?'

'Whichever pub they hung out in. He used to dip his toe in the waters, young Murray. And other bits of his anatomy. See which way the wind was blowing or the tide was turning.'

'Is that how Lambastier would have met him?'

'I'm not doing all your homework for you,' Fullalove said.

'Is this dealer to the stars still around?'

'Sure. Still. The shooting stars have shot to celebrity status. The meteorites have showered their sparks and buried themselves in the desert. The tourists on temporary artistic visas have relocated to the choicer suburbs. But Luke remains. He was smart. He kept away from the hard stuff. Never dealt heroin or cocaine or amphetamines. Just marijuana. Not even hashish. No customs and import issues, no playing in the big league. So never got busted. Apparently.'

'How do you know all this?'

Fullalove smiled, a sad smile of amused reproach. 'How do you think I know? Have an informed guess.'

'He's still dealing.'

Fullalove nodded.

'And you...?'

'Once in a while I drop by. The occasional drought or whatever.'

'So he's your regular dealer. Or one of them.'

'More of a back-up,' Fullalove said

'And he was Lambastier's dealer?'

'You make him sound like a card sharp. But yes, if I were to make an informed guess, yes.'

'You've got his number?'

'And his address. He doesn't like phone calls.'

'So what's he do? Fill me in?'

'He's a dealer.'

'Yes, I get that. But what's his cover story? Or is he full-time?'

'Pretty much, I'd reckon. Though he always had some part-time cover job or other. You know, bookshop manager, sales rep, festival organizer, supply teacher, buying and selling art at auctions, movie extra. He hung around the scene getting bits of work here and there. Gave him an identity. Gave him access. But all temporary stuff, none of it ever lasted or he never stuck with it. Whether he wanted it like that or he just got fired I don't know. Never seemed to be worried, anyway.'

'You knew him well?'

'No, I just drop by when I need a deal once in a while. You know, like bottle shops, you don't want them knowing how much you're drinking so you spread your custom around. No, not my scene. I didn't ever like that sit round the kitchen table and tell us all the gossip number.'

'Unless it's your kitchen table.'

'No mate, no way. You want a quiet talk, go outside, walk in a park. Or a cemetery, even better. Neutral territory. Keep changing the venue. Keep walking, preferably, avoid park benches.'

'Why's that?' Plant asked. As if he didn't know.

'You know why. Basic horticulture. Avoid the bugs.'

'Didn't he worry about that?'

'I don't know. But I did.'

'How big a scene was it?'

'Big enough. Drop in before the pub. Or after the pub. Or instead of the pub. Poets and filmmakers and academics and journalists, all the young chattering class in their larval stage, before they grew into fully-formed shell-backed ticks.'

'Did he write?'

'Probably. A lot of them did. Wrote a few stories or poems. Some went on to become advertising copywriters or solicitors or radio producers or semi-celebrities like Lambastier. Some didn't.'

'And he didn't.'

'No idea. No idea what he does or what his aspirations are. He might be writing the great Australian novel. Or epic poem. Or he could just be sitting on the couch watching Fox news on the telly. Or doing both. No idea. You'll just have to ask him when you see him. Subtly, of course, though I have no need to tell you that, do I, I hope not.'

'No, you don't.'

'Thought not. Sorry about that.'

'No worries.'

'Are you sure?'

'Yes, I'm sure.'

'Cool,' Fullalove said.

Plant let him have the last word.

But it was never the last word with Fullalove. There was always more. 'Those were the days,' he sighed.

'I thought you said you didn't like the scene.'

'I said it wasn't my scene. I found the poets hard to take.'

'But they weren't all poets?'

'No, thank heavens. They don't need to be. Just one's enough. No, Luke collected all sorts. Like the pub. He collected a lot of them from the pub, in fact. They were all young then. In their first jobs. Research assistants to politicians. Cadet journalists. Film reviewers. Art teachers. Trainee radio producers. Gophers in the movie business. This was when the suburb was becoming gentrified. First of all the students and bohemians moved in because it was run down and cheap. They ethnically cleansed it for the moneyed middle class to buy in and take over. Some of the bohemians and former students stayed on. Most moved. Luke was one who stayed. And his world moved away. Some would come back to pick up a deal. But the days of just sitting around raving on were fading. Now you dropped by, paid for a deal and left, pretty well straight away. No more sitting round the kitchen table.'

'And was Lambastier round that kitchen table in the good old days?'

'That's why I'm telling you this,' Fullalove said. 'What do you think I'm doing, composing a *Daily Telegraph* "Remember when" feature? Come to think of it, that wouldn't be a bad idea. "Remember when we used to sit round the kitchen table in Balmain with a bowl of marijuana heads, Zig-Zag cigarette papers and a packet of Drum rolling tobacco in front of us, discussing art and life and movies and sex and politics? What a time we had, inhibition released by the dope and booze, competing in telling the most discreditable anecdotes or promoting the latest extreme political position or arguing over the latest European movie? Books on the kitchen table, coffee-table books, art, architecture, classic cars, comix, books you normally didn't see around, American small press and instant remainder titles."'

'Why not write it? Give it a go.'

'You reckon I'd get away with it?'

'If you left out the bowl of heads.'

'That would miss the point though, wouldn't it?'

'Pretty much,' Plant agreed.

Chapter Sixteen

'What's his number then?' Plant asked.

'Whose number?'

'Your dealer to the stars.'

'Luke? He doesn't like phone calls. For obvious reasons. Never know when you're being listened to in his line of business.'

'So he's not going to like it if someone he's never met just fronts up on his doorstep.'

'Probably not.'

'Maybe you could give him a call.'

'He doesn't like calls.'

'So maybe you could front up with me.'

'Maybe I could,' Fullalove conceded. 'Maybe you could buy me a deal for my trouble.'

It was an unremarkable, rickety weatherboard cottage amidst other unremarkable weatherboard cottages in a narrow lane in Balmain. All with the barred windows of inner-city living. Plant imagined having to get out in a hurry if there was a fire or a home invasion. Whether it was worth the forty thousand dollars Fullalove said Luke gave for it or the two million he claimed it was worth now, the fact remained that it was an old weatherboard shack fronting the street with no views, no grounds. But yes, it had been a shrewd investment. Brilliant, yes brilliant. But would you ever want to live there? Not Plant. Not now the call of the wild lantana had got to him.

The door opened and a heavily-built man stood there, holding onto the door frame with one arm as if to prop himself up from falling down. Overweight, if you took the health-police view of things. Coarse blue work-shirt stretched tight over his belly, belly hanging over belted jeans that looked, insofar as it was possible to see, about to burst open. Out of breath, too, though doing his best to conceal that. A lifetime of smoking. Dealers' disease. Some dealers were said not to use their own product but Plant had never met one. His hair was full and grizzled. Unkempt, if you accepted the language of the kempt. Needed a shave, too, but maybe that was inner-city chic.

'I've brought a friend,' Fullalove said.

'Come in then,' Luke said, opening the door wide, beckoning them in, urgent hand and arm gestures, don't just stand there attracting the attention of the neighbours, was that it? Or was he finding the effort of standing exhausting?

'Sit down,' he ordered, closing the door, gesturing into the house.

It was a long, low narrow room. Originally it might have been two, even three small rooms reaching to the back of the cottage. Now it was like an art space. And art hung on the walls, or what passed for art, minimalist stuff that could have been originals or could have been prints, the shock of the no longer new. Art books on the single bookshelf. Pricey ones. None of them cheap. Maybe he'd souvenired them when he worked in the book trade. Remainders. Instant remainders, marketed as remainders. Not much obvious literary stuff. A shrine to visual culture with a disturbing suggestion of a funeral parlour. Maybe it was the Ray Charles organ track that was giving that impression.

'You want field-grown organic or hydroponic?' Luke asked, no messing around.

'Field-grown if you've got it,' Fullalove said. 'And my friend here will take the same.'

Luke produced electronic scales and fiddled around with them. Where, oh where were the brass weights of yesteryear? Bring back the jewellers' scales, and the abacus, and the magic of the bazaar. He weighed a couple of plastic bags of heads. Presumably they had been packed before and he was just checking. Unless this was part of the theatre of supply, everything coming pre-packed these days ready to put on the shelves for self-service, but open display self-service not the way dealers generally preferred to do business.

'Right,' Luke barked after Plant had handed over cash payment. He gestured towards the door. 'Off you go.'

No sitting round the kitchen table. Fullalove was right about that.

'The reason we're here,' Fullalove began.

Luke looked at him in some puzzlement. 'Was to buy dope,' he answered for them, all pretty self-evident. His arm still gesturing towards the door.

'Liz Lambastier,' Plant said, no time to prevaricate or to introduce the subject circuitously. Just get in the details promptly before they were out on the street.

Luke gave a slow, saurian smile.

'Is she back in town?'

'In a manner of speaking,' Fullalove offered.

'She's dead, actually,' Plant said.

'Oh, yeah, so she is.'

'You knew her?'

'Saw her around.'

'Around where?'

Luke looked puzzled.

'Like around,' he said.

'What, the pub?'

'Yeah, the pub.'

'She ever come round here?'

'Yeah, she'd come round here.'

He grinned, suggestively maybe, except that Plant wasn't sure what he might have been suggesting.

'My friend here is looking for an unpublished manuscript of Lambastier's,' Fullalove said.

Plant looked down the room. It probably wasn't called a room. It was more like a beer hall in an Anglo-Saxon epic. An imitation warehouse conversion. An ersatz New York loft. The artwork on the wall. And the overall neatness of it. It spoke painting rather than print. A long central table, but free of books or magazines. A clear glass bowl in the centre, empty of fruit and matches and cigarette papers, empty of everything, just proclaiming its empty self, not even allowed a functionalism, unless proclaiming absence was its function. Not the sort of place you would expect to find a missing manuscript.

'Why would I have it?' Luke asked.

'No, I wasn't expecting you to have it,' Plant said. 'It's just that Fullalove says you knew the scene. Were sort of central to it, as I understand.'

He waited for Luke to preen, but Luke was not one to give much away, in expression or in movement. His characteristic was immobility, if anything. Relic of the stoned age.

'So you never bartered a deal for a manuscript?'

Luke looked at him blankly. Blank amazement, maybe.

'What do you think I am?'

'You never traded a deal for an artwork?' Fullalove asked.

'For an artwork, maybe.'

'But not a manuscript,' Plant persisted.

'Why would I want a manuscript? She was a lousy poet anyway.'

'A travel manuscript. A memoir.'

'Not interested.'

'I'm trying to track down this book her sister says she wrote and never published.'

'How would her sister know?' Luke asked. 'They didn't speak to each other.'

'Is that so?'

'So she said. Hated each other. Sister's straight as a die. Marriage. Husband. Divorce. Money. All the shit Liz hated.'

'Ah well, she's on the case now. She reckons her sister wrote this last book before she died and it never got published.'

'Doubt it,' Luke said. 'She wasn't in any state to write anything last time I saw her.'

'You saw her then?'

'She came round a couple of times. Tragic.'

'What was wrong?'

'She said it was something she'd picked up in Asia somewhere. But who knows?'

'You think it wasn't?'

'Looked like your terminal junkie to me. But who knows? Could have been Hep-C. Or AIDS. Looked pretty sick to me. Can't imagine she was writing anything in that state. Past it. A human wreck.'

He said it with a certain satisfaction, Plant felt. Another meteorite crashed to earth. Another talent burnt out.

'And you wouldn't know anyone she might've given a manuscript to for safe keeping, say?'

'Why would she?'

'Well, it's not in her papers in the State Library.'

'Maybe it doesn't exist.'

'I'm not sure it does,' Plant said. 'I'm just checking out places where it might be.'

'Well, it's not here,' Luke said. 'Bloody woman.'

Plant looked up. Interrogatively.

'Tried to blackmail me, didn't she?'

Plant waited.

'Twisted my arm to give a donation to some women's refuge she was mixed up in. Said I could either give her a percentage of the profits I was making dealing, or she'd dob me in.'

'Dob you in?'

'Yeah.'

'What, to the cops?'

'No, give us a break. She said she'd put it in some pissy article she was writing. Male chauvinism in the drug trade. How I was a big time dealer who made a fortune out of her and her friends and refused to donate to the cause. If I refused.'

'Did she?'

'No, I paid up.'

'So she was really into the women's movement back then. Like seriously committed. Setting up a refuge.'

'Believe what you want,' Luke said. 'I think she was mainly into giving me a hard time. That was her idea of feminism. Giving people like me a hard time.'

'People like you?' Fullalove said.

'Men.'

Luke rolled up a number and lit it and sucked on it and inhaled and coughed and choked like he'd been doing for fifty years. Always inhaling that first blast too deeply, too long, too much, and always coughing and spluttering, how to wake up in the morning, and at set intervals throughout the day. Fullalove held out a hand to take the joint from him.

'She used to hang round the poetry scene back then,' Luke said. 'Tried to be one of the boys. Bunch of wankers now. But in those days they were...'

He seemed lost for words.

'Real poets?' Plant offered.

'Yeah,' Luke agreed. 'Full-on fighting poets.'

'Fighting?'

'Like fighting cocks. In every sense.'

'And she was in the barnyard with them.'

Fullalove made cock-a-doodle-doo noises.

'It was serious stuff,' Luke said. 'Poetry mattered. They fought for it.'

'Like they were in Vietnam or Nicaragua,' Fullalove offered.

'Sure, man.'

Plant grunted.

'Great,' he said.

'They mounted a coup. Took over this poetry magazine. Stacked the meeting, signed up members in the pub and dragged them along. Kicked out the editor and the board.'

'Sounds fun.'

'Actually it was fucking tedious. All those committee meetings.

Procedural motions. Straw votes. Secret ballots. Some of them were really into that whole fucking business, should've stayed in the ALP stacking the local branch.'

'What was the point?'

'Get hold of a magazine that would publish your stuff.'

'And did you?'

'Me? I was just a casual observer.'

'Barracking from the sidelines,' Fullalove said.

'Well, a man's got to have a bit of fun.'

'And Lambastier published her stuff there?'

'I guess so. Till she moved on.'

'Moved on?' Plant asked.

'She got caught up with Murray Brittan, didn't she?'

'And he started publishing her?'

'And the rest,' Luke said, knowingly.

'Who else?'

'What else, more to the point,' Luke said, his peremptoriness softening at the appeals of gossip. Plant waited. But the promise was not fulfilled. It remained a mere suggestion. High postmodernism. Beyond representation. In the end just the trace of innuendo.

'Is he still around?' Plant asked. Casually. As casually as he could contrive.

'You can see his chauffeur-driven limo whisk him along Darling Street most mornings if you get up early enough.'

'I should probably talk to him.'

'About Lambastier?'

'Yes.'

'Give him a call.'

'Not sure a call would work.'

'Go and see him then.'

'Sure. How do I do that? Knock on his door and get a flea in my ear?'

'Go along to his fundraising next week.'

'I thought he was a billionaire. Why does he need to raise funds?'

'One of his writers or lawyers or something is standing for parliament. Or pre-selection. Or something. So Murray's opened his mansion.'

'Nice of him.'

Luke didn't take the bait. 'Yeah,' he agreed.

'Why doesn't he just put up the money? Rather than have his house trashed.'

'He never opens the house. Just the grounds. On the waterfront.'

'Still...'

'The look of the thing. To make it look like there's a support base,' Fullalove said.

'And can anyone go? Or is it invitation only?'

'Why not? It's a fundraiser. The more the merrier,' Luke said.

'And it's not exclusive? You're sure?'

'Of course I'm sure. I've known him for years. I'll take you along if you want. Drop by here next Saturday and I'll get you in.'

'A pleasure doing business with you,' Plant said.

Chapter Seventeen

Plant called in on Luke early Saturday afternoon. He was showered, brushed, trim. They both were. But reasonably at ease with it.

'Another deal? Shit man, you got through that already? Good thing you haven't got emphysema. Yet. Come in, man, don't fuck around on the doorstep.'

Plant gave his desperado smile.

'Bush-grown organic or hydroponic special?' Luke asked.

'What's special about the hydroponic?'

'All the hydroponic's special. So's the bush-grown organic.'

'So it's like a brand name.'

'If you like. Which do you want?'

There was a certain peremptoriness in Luke's responses. Dealer to the stars.

'Bush if you've got it. Is it really bush-grown? Free-range?'

'Probably. Who knows? But it's organic.'

'Is it really?'

'Smoke it and see.'

'Actually,' Plant said, 'I came round for Murray Brittan's fundraising.'

'Oh shit, yeah, sure, forgot. So do you want a deal or not?'

'Sure. While I'm here.'

Luke fiddled around with his scales, checked the weight of the deal, handed it over, took the cash.

'Right man,' he said, 'let's go.'

Murray Brittan's harbour-side mansion, or one of them, since he probably had a number scattered around, was one of the old sea captains' houses on the Birchgrove waterfront with a view down to the Harbour Bridge. He was still publishing. The magazine Lambastier had written her first travel pieces for had died but he'd moved into books early on, a spin-off from the magazine with its eager contributors, all with the odd manuscript or three on hand should the chance of publication arise. Which with Murray it did. Though most of it now, the book publishing, was basically badge engineering, buying an already edited and designed and formatted book from the USA or UK and sticking his imprint on the title page, verso and spine. But his interests stretched far wider than publishing and into far more lucrative areas, moving in and out of what was hot, tax-credit movie schemes, mobile phones, travel, high-end restaurants, property, resorts, mining. Publishing had allowed him to peddle influence, take on a bit of token local talent, do favours to up-and-coming assets, access to a profile through the magazine and a platform to promote whatever political or economic line he was involved in promoting. Which he was still doing, presumably, with this fundraiser, even though the magazine no longer existed.

The terraced grounds sloped down to the water, a gentle, grassed expanse, punctuated with huge urns and amphorae and such like ornamentation, stone and terracotta or, for all Plant knew, poured concrete. He could have asked the dealer to the stars who may have known, an eye for the aesthetic of objects. But he didn't. A jetty reached out into the water and a large motor yacht was moored there. Could have asked the dealer to the stars about that too, is this the sort of vessel that heads out through the Heads and makes rendezvous with freighters from Colombia or wherever, or picks up floating cargo with the aid of electronic tracking devices and all that? The sort of thoughts that conspicuous wealth inspired in Plant's head. He let them stay in his head, unvocalized. Along with his speculations about the yacht's cost. He had no idea. Not quite as much as the house was his best estimate.

'This is where the readings use to be held,' Luke said, gesturing with his arm outstretched, the Boyhood of Raleigh, learning to lisp in numbers at the water's edge. A good poet, too, Sir Walter, as well as being the man who introduced smoking to the Anglo-Saxon world. Where would Luke have been without that? Eating the stuff, or drinking it as bhang.

'That's where they used to read from,' Luke said, indicating one of the terraces. 'And that's where they used to throw things from.'

'Throw things?'

'At the poets. Empty beer cans and stuff.'

Luke introduced Plant to Murray Brittan, and added a bit of solicitous concern. 'You don't have a drink. Can I get you one?'

'First thing they told me about entering politics,' Murray said, 'was never be photographed with a drink in your hand or a funny hat on your head. Or vice versa for that matter.'

He was bare-headed, good head of grey hair, seersucker suit, open-necked pale blue shirt, brown moccasins. In his sixties. Or, not impossibly, a decade older but fit. One of those trim, stocky men of medium height, or less, who desire and emanate power.

'Are you entering politics?' Plant asked.

'Have I ever left?' Murray asked back.

Plant looked puzzled.

'There are more ways of entering politics than getting elected,' Murray said.

Luke laughed. Not exactly sycophantically. But getting there.

'So, Mr Plant,' Murray said, 'what's your game?'

'My game? Like big game shooting? Or polo? Roulette?'

Murray smiled with one of those smiles that are not at all a smile, totally fake. Like so much else about him, Plant assumed.

'You know what I mean, Mr Plant. Luke tells me you wish to speak to me about Liz Lambastier. It is good to meet you at last but this is not the best time to talk.'

'At last' Plant repeated to himself, reflectively, as reflectively as he could manage in mid-conversation.

'Perhaps you should come here tomorrow. Sunday morning. Say ten a.m. That way we'll have the day ahead of us. Though I don't imagine that we shall need that long.'

'Sure,' Plant said.

'We could go out on the harbour,' Murray smiled. 'Or beyond, even,' he added, smiling even more disturbingly.

'That would be nice,' Plant said, lying through his teeth, trying not to grit them before he could get his reply out.

Murray laid a hand on Plant's shoulder.

'Tomorrow,' he said.

'Tomorrow,' Plant agreed.

'Tomorrow and tomorrow and tomorrow,' Murray intoned, striding off to deal with his next problem.

Felix Hacker greeted Plant warily, a glass of wine in one hand and his fingers squeezing into some partially-eaten fine-food concoction in the other.

'How are your researches?' he asked.

'Still searching,' Plant said.

'The magazines,' Hacker intoned. 'The magazines. That's where you should be looking. That's where she did her best work. And it was good, let me tell you.'

'Didn't she collect it all into her books?'

'Nothing wrong with that,' Hacker said.

'Not at all,' Plant agreed. 'But I don't know if there's anything there that she didn't collect.'

'Could be. No way to know without looking,' Hacker said. 'That was her lifeblood, the magazines. That was the lifeblood for all of us. There they were for three centuries. Everyone who was anyone wrote for the magazines. Dickens, Trollope, Henry James, Conan Doyle, P. G. Wodehouse, Scott Fitzgerald. That's where the talent was, that's where the money was. *The Strand*, *The Saturday Evening Post*, *Harper's*, *New Yorker*. And she was part of it. She started off here with us. And then she went international.

Cosmopolitan, *Vanity Fair*, *Vogue*.

'Global,' Plant agreed, nation and national and international rather archaic terms now that capitalism was achieving its domination over national interests. 'And it got her into television.'

'In those days,' Hacker assured him, 'print led the way. Television fed off print. The talk shows and the morning shows fed off the print culture and Liz was in print in the right places at the right times. And that's a world that has pretty well gone.'

Plant nodded sadly.

'The tragedy is,' Hacker surged ahead, monologue his preferred mode, 'why would anybody be interested in her now? Even if this book you're looking for is any good, there wouldn't be any money in it. You couldn't sell serial rights, there's nowhere left to sell them to. Pretty well. Effectively. Not to put too gloomy a picture on it, it's all over.'

'I guess so,' Plant agreed.

'The only things keeping newsagents going is lottery tickets. As soon as the supermarkets get the go-ahead to sell them, the magazines will be finished. Advertising's all moved to the internet. There's nothing to keep magazines and newspapers afloat. That's why Murray's going down.'

'Is he?'

'Of course he is. All old media is. He's finished. Just a matter of when. Could be the last time you'll be walking these lawns.'

'This is the first time, actually,' Plant said.

'There you are then,' Hacker said. 'Now for the vast emptiness of the future.'

He seemed to enjoy saying it. Years of minatory editorials behind him awaiting their final culmination.

'All over now, anyway,' Hacker assured him. 'The barbarians are within the walls.'

Plant nodded some more.

Hacker swallowed the chunk of food he had been holding and gestured with his empty hand. Plant looked to where he was pointing.

'Vandals, Goths and Visigoths,' Hacker said, rifling the word-hoard of the old print culture, the pre-print culture even. 'Here she comes, swinging her wrecking ball and laying all to waste. The black widow of the worldwide web.'

He licked his fingers.

'All yours,' he said, gesturing, leaving, departing, pretty well scuttling. He faded away in a flurry of words, vanishing out of earshot, out of sight, like the lost world of the magazines.

Chapter Eighteen

Angela Dark hove into view. Like a stately galleon. Or a cruise ship, maybe. One of those nearly too big to pass beneath the Harbour Bridge. *News from the Dark Side* in person. Cyberspace made flesh. All carmine lipstick, raven hair, funerals-and-interviews dark suit. Making it clear she was here for work, not pleasure, in case anyone had any other impression. The red shoes were part of the work-wear outfit, the red and the black, the colours of anarchy, as befitted a libertarian with a sense of style and a media figure requiring ready recognisability.

'Plant!' she said.

He admitted it.

'I cannot tell a lie,' he said.

'That's another one to begin with.'

Plant shrugged.

'What are you doing here?' she asked.

'Partying,' he said. 'What about you?'

'You're the investigator, you tell me.'

'Scavenging gossip for your oily rag?'

She shook her head.

'How's your investigation going, dare I ask?' she asked.

'What investigation?'

'Oh, we are being coy, aren't we? Your inquiries into the late unlamented Liz Lambastier.'

'What about her?'

'A flock of little birds tells me you've been making some inquiries about her. Oh, sorry, you're not an inquiry agent though, are you, my mistake. Conducting some research into her *œuvre*, is that better?'

'No.'

'Is that a no denoting your lack of progress or an indication that you've been taken off the case?'

'It's a no meaning it's not better.'

'What's not better?'

'Forget it,' Plant said.

'Can't do that. I'm on your case, Plant, you'd better come clean.'

'Or?'

'Or you can go online and see the next *News from the Dark Side*.'

'No, thank you.'

'Wow, politeness, what provoked that?'

He said nothing. Clearly best to say nothing if what he was saying was sounding polite to Angela Dark.

'I thought it might be in our mutual interest to have a chat,' she said.

'Sounds unlikely.'

'Doesn't it! But there you are.'

'What about?'

'Liz Lambastier, of course.'

'Did you know her?'

'Did I know her? Fucking cow.'

Luke gave a guffaw.

It sounded promising. More than promising. Why hadn't he thought of contacting Angela Dark before? Spontaneous memory loss, evidently. A bit of a worry. Unless it was simply repression, denial, a way of coping with the world's unpleasantness, a self-protective reflex saving him from ever thinking about people like Angela Dark let alone voluntarily contacting them, probably a good thing, not something to worry about at all, maybe even something to cultivate.

'So what's your interest in Lambastier?' she asked.

'What's yours?'

'I asked first.'

'Ah well, as the good book puts it, the first shall be last and the last shall be first.'

'Has anybody ever told you you're a pain, Plant?'

'Possibly,' he conceded. He gave a smile of irritating satisfaction. Certainly other people had told him they found it irritating.

'All right,' she said, 'all right. My interest is in what you're interested in.'

'And what's that?'

'That's my interest. In finding out what it is.'

'Ah,' Plant said. 'So you have no interest other than inquiring into my interest.'

'That's what I said.'

'You're not running your own investigation.'

'Only into you.'

'Into me?'

'Into your interest in her.'

He reflected. It was probably true.

'He's trying to track down an unpublished manuscript of hers,' Luke said.

Angela groaned.

'Spare us,' she said. 'Do we have to have another?'

'I'm looking,' Plant said.

'But you haven't found it?'

'No.'

'Well that's something.'

'Not yet.'

She groaned some more.

'Have you looked in Mitchell Library?'

'Nothing there.'

'I thought her papers were there. All two thousand untouched boxes. Waiting in vain for a biographer.'

'They are. But no unpublished manuscript.'

'Try the university, then.'

‘The university?’

‘The university library. We had a policy of building up women’s resources. We got them to buy all sorts of material, correspondence, papers, magazines, newsletters, flyers for meetings, minutes for meetings. She could have sold it to them. They had the funds at one time. Back then. Or donated it for a tax credit. She wouldn’t have given it to them for free, you can bet that.’

He thanked her. It would have been profusely, except that she cut him off.

‘Forget it. Don’t even know why I bothered to tell you.’

‘You’re not a fan of hers.’

‘You can say that again.’

‘You’re not a...’

‘Stow it, Plant. No, I’m not a fan.’

‘You knew her.’

‘Unfortunately.’

‘Tell me,’ he said. ‘If it will make you feel better,’ he added, solicitously, as solicitously as he could manage.

Angela glared at him.

‘This is not for publication,’ she said.

‘You’re the journalist, not me.’

‘Yeah, well, not for want of trying, was it? So don’t use this story as a way of getting back in there.’

‘In where?’

‘Forget it, Plant. I just want your fucking agreement that what I’m going to tell you is off the record.’

‘Of course.’

‘It better be,’ she said.

‘Of course.’

‘You too,’ she said to Luke.

‘Of course.’

‘I had this friend. Still have, for that matter. My friend gets pregnant. Being brought up a good Christian girl she decides to have the baby. She doesn't want to see the guy again. One-night stand stuff. Tells him nothing. But her mother goes ape, and fucking Lambastier, who was a so-called friend of my friend, goes and tells my friend's mother who the father is and the mother gets onto his family and, to cut a long story short, the families force my friend and the guy to get married which is as you might imagine a fucking disaster. Lasts a couple of years or so until they call it quits and my friend gets out of it and regains a life of her own. That's Lambastier. Champion of women's rights. Internationally acclaimed feminist. Fucking cow.

'Lambastier was just a narcissistic, interfering bitch. Forget feminism, forget human rights, forget her travels in the Third World, she had no fucking interest in anything except herself. A full-on malignant narcissist who fucked up people's lives. As long as she was centre stage she didn't care what she said or did. She just liked pushing people around. Telling everyone else what to do. Pointing out what they were doing wrong. All off the top of her head, she never stopped to think what she was saying or what she was doing.'

'So she wasn't a true feminist in your opinion?'

'True? She wasn't a true anything. True is not a word you use in relation to Liz Lambastier.'

'And feminist?'

'Liz Lambastier? You've got to be joking. Sure, she waved the feminist flag. But the only thing she was seriously promoting was herself. Basically it was all about her. She was an opportunist. Feminism came along at the right time in her career trajectory through the arts and the media and eventually via bonking into banking or whatever, money anyway. She was poised to profit by it. Forget equal pay for working women, people like Liz didn't want equality with anybody, they just wanted the big bucks and the celebrity status. Feminism suited people like her. She rode the waves – confrontation, separatism, lesbianism, political correctness. Whatever the latest fashionable development, she was there. But primarily she was just an unprincipled hack, a presenter, a performer, superficial, facile. Not a thinker. Not a real journalist. Just a fucking evil egomaniac.'

'Have you ever written this?' Plant asked.

'Are you crazy?'

'She's dead. She wouldn't sue.'

'I'm not about to give ammunition to all those disgusting, misogynistic, drunken old men you hang out with.'

'You want me to write it up?'

'Don't even think it. This is off the record, right?'

'Chatham House rules.'

'My rules,' she said. 'My friend's still alive. And the child. I'm telling you this so you have some real idea of what you're dealing with. But I'm not about to go public with it. And nor are you.'

'Not if you say not.'

She gave him one of the jagged-edged steely looks she had cultivated and perfected.

'Are there other people who feel like this about Lambastier?'

'Anyone who ever dealt with her, I imagine.'

'I hadn't encountered it.'

'Then you've been talking to the wrong people.'

'I'm just looking for this manuscript. I'm not interviewing her friends and acquaintances.'

'You can forget friends,' Angela said. 'You won't find any of them.'

He didn't say he'd found a couple of people who didn't speak ill of her. No point debating the issue. It wasn't relevant to his search, anyway, as far as he could see.

'Thanks anyway,' he said. 'And if you happen to hear about any unpublished manuscript...'

'I'll make sure it's destroyed,' she assured him.

She didn't add 'I'm joking.' She probably wasn't. She sounded deadly serious. It didn't seem like the appropriate time to argue the issue. Though it was a bit of a worry.

'What about Murray Brittan?' he asked. Rival media. Who knew what response it might elicit?

'What about him?'

'Lambastier used to write for him, didn't she?'

'Why wouldn't she? Usual fascist media pig.'

'Didn't you work for him once?'

'You want to be a journalist in this country, there's not a lot of choice in who you work for. Doesn't mean you have to like them to work for them. And it's up to you how far you follow their line. There mightn't be any other possibility around, there mightn't be any choice, but it's still up to you how far you roll over. And if you were worried about holding down your job, rolling over might seem the easiest way to go. It's certainly worked for a lot of the fuckers.'

'Is that a yes or a no?'

'Work it out,' she said.

'But Lambastier worked for him.'

'Like I said, it's the business. You don't have to like them to work for them. Or to fuck them.'

'Did you have to fuck them to work for them?'

'I don't think Liz worried about who she worked for or who she fucked or how she got work. She'd work for anyone who was mug enough to pay her. She didn't get that much. Not regularly. She made it look like she was in demand. She was a smart operator. She sort of came and went in the fame game. She'd be up there with some book she was promoting or reporting on something and then she'd have disappeared. She played it well. She made it look like she was off somewhere investigating but it was just that no one was hiring her, she wasn't getting any work, hadn't written anything else, hadn't got a regular slot. She was good at making it look like it was all her choice, like she was fucking condescending to front up and write once in a while, when the reality was she was scrabbling for work. But, you know, she hung in there.'

'With Murray.'

'Till his magazine folded.'

'And then?'

'Who knows? Who cares? She was out of the country. She always gave the impression she was writing for all these overseas papers. But who knows? Who ever saw them? Who ever checked?'

'So she was a fraud.'

'No, she wasn't a fraud. Not exactly. She had talent. But you've got to ask, how did she use that talent? Probably as far as it went. You know, you hear talk about people betraying their gifts, but I think most people just write at their own level and there's no choice about it. She was just what she was. She had that characteristic of successful people, media people, actors, of being whatever the reader or viewer wants them to be, like a chameleon. It's not a case of people like her betraying a cause and selling out. They never nail themselves to any cause, if you look closely. But they always manage to seem simpatico to a whole lot of people. People who probably wouldn't agree with each other. It's a gift. But it needs careful cultivation. She was good at it.'

Chapter Nineteen

Ghostly Sperrit came into focus, stomach well to the fore, rivalling Luke's, dressed as ever in his single-breasted shiny blue blazer, baggy grey trousers, grubby white shirt and what could have been his old school tie, wherever that might have been. He emerged from amongst the guests and supplicants, a beer in one hand and his other arm draped proprietorially around a female person, holding her in bondage, or holding her to support himself. It was the girl from the library, Sasha, Plant realized as they came closer.

'Ghostly!' Angela called out.

Ghostly waved his glass of beer, not too vigorously, nothing spilled.

'Comrades!' he intoned fruitily.

Plant offered the suggestion of a smile.

'So what crimes against humanity are you two investigating today?' Ghostly asked, in measured, sepulchral tones.

Since he'd asked, Plant told him. Who knew what Ghostly might know, sometime political speechwriter, occasional journalist and once-in-a-while filmmaker?

'Liz Lambastier.'

'Had her on the back seat of Murray's Bentley,' he said.

'Thank you for that useful information,' Angela said.

'Bet you say that about all the girls,' Sasha said, removing Ghostly's arm from her shoulders, but he put it back and tightened his hold.

'If you're up for it,' Ghostly said. 'The car's in the garage.'

'I'll pass,' Sasha said. 'But thanks all the same,' she added sweetly.

'How did Murray take that?' Plant asked

'Pissed him off no end.'

'Sexual jealousy is a terrible thing.'

'No, it wasn't that. Stained the leather seat. Really pissed him off.'

'*Coitus interruptus*, was it?' Angela asked. 'Too cheap to use a condom. Or do you just like making a point of splashing your seed around?'

'No way of knowing it was mine,' Ghostly said. 'Could've been anyone's. Could've been Murray's. This was before DNA testing.'

'So what happened?' Plant asked.

'Nothing happened.'

'What an interesting anecdote,' Angela said.

'Not like his last stupid girlfriend,' Ghostly added.

'What happened to her?'

'He came home one afternoon and found her fucking the gardener.'

'And?'

'Out on her arse along with the gardener and my fucking movie treatment he was going to finance for her to star in.'

'What happened to the movie?'

'What happens to most movies. Nothing. I've written eighty-nine treatments and nine got made.'

'Mister almost ten percent,' Plant said.

'Pathetic, isn't it. I should've stuck to writing novels.'

'Didn't know you'd ever started,' Angela said.

'So what's the interest in Lambastier?' Ghostly asked.

'He's trying to find a missing manuscript of hers,' Sasha said.

'Why?' Ghostly asked.

'Hard to say,' Plant said. 'I just got asked.'

'Can't help you,' Ghostly said.

'But you knew her,' Plant said. 'Well, I suppose you must have. But did you…?'

Sasha cut across. '"Did you see much of her?" is what he wants to ask, and then you'll say, "All of her."'

Ghostly grinned.

Angela and Sasha did a bit of synchronized formation eye-rolling.

'So she never talked to you about what she was writing?' Plant persisted.

'Deeds not words,' Ghostly said. 'We are here to change the world, not talk about it.'

'Really,' Angela said.

'Yes.'

'Off you go then,' Sasha said.

He showed no signs of moving.

'Can't imagine why anybody would be interested,' Ghostly said.

'Why's that?'

'Why would they be? She wasn't really a writer. Some people are writers and they try and drum up some publicity to sell their books. Others are basically into the publicity and the books are just one way of getting it. The culture of narcissism. Institutionalized by the Australia Council. Promoted by what's left of the media and our national broadcaster and writers' festivals. With the focus always on the writer as personality rather than on the books. That's what's killed print culture, not the internet, comrade.'

'And Liz?'

'She was just your classic narcissist. Not a writer. Now she's dead and gone her books are dead and gone. They only served to get her television spots and magazine interviews and festival gigs. No lasting interest in them as books now she's gone. Even supposing anyone was interested in books any more.'

'And you, Ghostly?' Angela asked. 'Which are you? A would-be celebrity or a would-be writer?'

'Me?' Ghostly reflected. 'Oh, there's no would-be about me. I'll own up to both. You learn to take every opportunity in this business, comrade.'

'What business is that?' Plant asked. 'Were you the gardener, too? Doing a bit of odd-jobbing on the side?'

Ghostly seemed launched on denial, then checked himself. He settled into a silent smile of self-satisfaction. Years on the edge of the movie business had taught him to take any credit that might be on offer. And any sexual opportunity.

'Let's go to a movie,' he said to Sasha. 'I'll take you to a preview.'

She wrinkled her nose.

'I think I'll go to the library,' she said. 'Take out a novel.'

Ghostly shook his head wearily. The weirdness of women.

'How about you?' he asked Angela.

She laughed.

'We've been there, done that, thank you very much,' she said.

'I'll come,' Luke offered.

But Ghostly was already surveying the distant field.

'What library did you have in mind?' Plant asked Sasha.

'You're the expert. Make a suggestion,' she said.

Angela groaned and headed off. Ghostly lumbered after her.

'I didn't know you knew Ghostly,' Plant said to Sasha.

'Why should you?'

'No reason.'

Did he need to make an apology? Intrusiveness?

'I don't,' she said.

'You don't what?'

'Know Ghostly. Why's he called Ghostly?'

'Because his surname sounds like spirit. Or because he ghost-writes politicians' speeches and stuff. But who knows?'

'Who knows what?'

'Who knows anything? Why did you tell him I was looking for a manuscript?'

'Why not? Don't tell me this is classified information. Is it? Do I need a security clearance to talk to you? Is he called Ghostly because he's a spook?'

'Just a question.'

'Oh well, the more the merrier. The more people who know you're looking for it the better the chance of it turning up.'

'Maybe.'

'What, you don't want people like him to know? Think they might get in on the act? Like the gold rush or something?'

'It's hard to imagine.'

'I can imagine it,' Sasha said.

Chapter Twenty

'You want a lift?' Plant offered.

'Where are you going?'

'Wherever. Which library are you heading for?'

'Can't we just pass on the library?'

'Didn't you want to borrow a book?'

'What do you think?' Sasha asked.

'They're probably all shut by now, anyway,' he said.

'The books?'

'The libraries.'

'You think?'

Probably, he thought. He had no idea what time it was, let alone what time the local library might shut. They set off down the street and along the length of the next one.

'Is this your way of getting exercise, or are you too ashamed to park beside all the posh cars outside Murray's?' Sasha asked, as he stopped beside his no longer late-model pretty well bottom-of-the -line, Hyundai, economical, reliable, unobtrusive.

'It was the closest I could get.'

She gave a grunt, a sceptical one.

He clicked the remote on his key to unlock the doors and the car lights flashed. She got in without waiting for Plant to open the door for her. He was sitting beside her fastening his seat-belt when there was a tap on the window.

Luke peered through at them.

'Give us a lift, mate.'

No doubt it was fair to take Luke back since Plant had brought him and Luke had got him in. Fair, if annoying. Plant would have preferred just to be alone with Sasha. Fond hope. And probably a bad idea, anyway.

'Sure,' he said, without any great enthusiasm, indeed without enthusiasm at all. But Luke offered a reward. Or a bait. The 'want to come in for a smoke?' line.

'Sure,' Sasha said.

Luke rolled up a number and lit it and passed it round.

'Oh, I thought when you said come back for a smoke you meant a real smoke,' Sasha said, sucking on the joint while taking a pack of cigarettes from her jeans. Something which required much wriggling and a terrible risk of losing the joint, swallowing it or dropping it on the floor and crushing it, or just totally smoking it down to the roach, while Plant hung out there.

'You and Ghostly an item?' Luke asked.

'Me?' Sasha said. 'You've got to be joking.'

'You and Murray an item, then?'

'That's not even funny.'

'So it's you and Plant?'

'No way,' she said.

'Is that so?'

'That's so,' Plant assured him. A pity maybe. And did she have to be so adamant about it?

'So what brings you two together?'

Sasha looked across at Plant. Plant looked back. Neither said anything. But Plant sensed a moment of silent complicity, an unwillingness to be interrogated. Or to vocalize whatever it was that had brought them together. If they were together. Or might possibly be together in the future.

Luke waited for a reply. A grin hovering there, almost a grin, an annoying suggestion of a grin, alternating with the straight-faced impassivity of an immigration officer with the Balmain border police. Some sort of interrogator, anyway. Maybe just stoned and insensitive.

'I was checking out the Lambastier papers in the State Library. We bumped into each other.'

'Bump and grind,' Luke said. 'Cosy.'

They let that pass and ignored him.

'So are you going to check out the university library?' Luke tried again.

'I guess so,' Plant said.

'What university library?' Sasha asked.

'The one Angela Dark said had a feminist collection,' Luke said.

'Are you?' Sasha asked Plant.

'Could do,' Plant agreed, not revealing any high hopes or showing too much enthusiasm. He was becoming adept at that, high hopes and enthusiasm so often fading rather than being raised. Sad old world, he reflected.

'Is that a yes or a no?' she asked.

Plant smiled and took the joint Luke had passed her, what was left of it. Was this Luke's dealer-to-the-stars image of being a gentleman, observing quaint old customs like ladies first? Or had he been educated by feminists the hard way?

'Plant,' she snapped.

He smiled some more and inhaled. Inhaled some more. He was becoming quite experienced in withstanding interrogation techniques. Maybe not the advanced and enhanced ones. But those underway in a public place, and a dealer's living room qualified as a public place, he could handle. He was becoming quite experienced at a lot of things. Smiling seemed to help. And the dope certainly helped him to smile. Even before he'd inhaled, it seemed.

He offered a shrug.

'Some time, I guess,' he said

'What's it worth,' Luke asked, 'this book you're looking for? Couple of hundred grand?'

'That much?' Sasha said.

'I doubt it,' Plant said. 'Twenty thousand advance max, I'd imagine. Assuming someone would make an offer to publish it.'

'Got to be worth something,' Luke persisted.

'Not a lot,' Plant said.

'What happens if you can't find it?'

'Nothing,' Plant said. 'Can't find it. That's it.'

'Couldn't you fake it? It wouldn't be hard. Get a team on it. A couple of chapters each.'

It was like the 70s again. Bad boys with time on their hands. The enthusiasm for fakery outweighing any rational estimate of possible financial return. Like getting a poem into a women's only anthology. Or faking Aboriginal bark paintings.

Sasha gave a questioning look.

'I can't see the point,' Plant said.

'Money.'

'I can't see that there's going to be much demand for it.'

'So why're you looking for it?' Luke persisted.

'Her sister asked me to.'

'So what's her interest? She must think there's money in it.'

'I don't think so.'

'So why's she want it found? She's afraid there's some scandal? She wants to find it and burn it so it doesn't get published.'

'I don't think so,' Plant said again.

'What about her agent?' Luke asked. 'She must have had an agent.'

'Spare me,' Plant said.

'Have you checked her out?'

'She terrifies me,' Plant said.

Sasha snorted. 'Don't be a ridiculous patriarchal old tosser,' she said. 'Of course she doesn't terrify you. Man up.'

'I'd still rather not deal with her.'

'Why's that?' Luke asked.

'Unresolved Oedipal issues,' Sasha said.

'Wouldn't she have it? Or know where it is?' Luke persisted.

'If she had it she'd have got it published. And if she couldn't get it published she'd have sent it back.'

'Have you checked with her?'

Was it an innocent, obvious question, even a helpful suggestion? Or was it Luke checking on Plant?

'Plant!' Sasha prodded him.

The good thing about being stoned, or one of the things, and it was good dope, well, it got you stoned, narcotized, and that was the good thing about dope, it meant you could just sit there silent. Impassive, out of it, entranced. Like a fat seal.

'Honk, honk,' he went, but inwardly, silently.

'Didn't someone say she'd been burgled?' Luke asked.

'Agent Orange? Was that her?' Sasha asked. 'Did you hear that, Plant?'

'Hear what?' Plant asked, emerging from the ocean of the mind.

'Agent Orange was burgled.'

'Hear it where? On the news? I shouldn't have thought it rated news coverage. Though she's got her media contacts. But you'd've thought she'd use them to kill the story. Bad for business, getting burgled. Like a bank losing your money. Not a good look. Where did you hear it?'

'Can't remember,' Luke said. 'Someone must've mentioned it.'

'One of your steady stream of visitors,' Plant suggested.

'You get a lot of visitors?' Sasha asked.

'Do you?' Luke asked.

'Where did you hear it?' Plant asked Sasha.

'I don't know that I did.'

'You said "was that her?"'

'Did I?'

'Yes.'

'Must be the dope,' she said. '*Déjà vu.*'

They sat there at the bare, scrubbed pine table, the empty glass bowl, the silicone-coated wooden floor free of any carpets or rugs, minimalist expressions of artistic taste on the walls, the clarity and emptiness of a western European movie of a certain era, preserved in aspic or isinglass or frozen in time in some cryogenic procedure.

'How about some music?' Sasha asked.

'When I play music I play it to listen to,' Luke said. 'When I talk to people I like to hear them.'

'Get a hearing aid, why don't you?' Sasha suggested.

'I'm not going deaf.'

'Most people your age are,' she said.

When in doubt, roll another number. Luke rolled another, lit it, sucked on it, inhaled, and passed it on.

'So what were you doing at Murray's party?' Plant asked Sasha.

'I'm a party animal.'

'Is that so?'

'Sure is.'

'Party animal rather than party girl?'

'Girl in that context is unacceptably discriminatory,' she said. 'Don't you think?'

'I'm a vegetarian,' Plant said. 'I'm happy with animals.'

'Bestiality,' Luke suggested.

'So?' Sasha asked.

'So how come you were invited?' he persisted.

'I wasn't.'

'But you went anyway.'

'Yes.'

'Did you know the candidate?'

'The what?'

'The person the fundraiser was for.'

'The fundraiser?'

'The party.'

'What was it raising funds for?'

'For whoever it was to get into parliament.'

'Oh.'

'Did you know them?'

'Oh. No. Do you?'

'No.'

She laughed.

There was a silence as Plant thought about formulating another question.

'So how come you were there?' he tried.

'My aunt.'

'Go on.

'She used to know Murray.'

'She and Liz.'

'Yes.'

'And?'

'So that's how.'

'What, she gets invited and you stand in for her?'

'Sort of. Why not?'

'So Murray remembers his old friends.'

'It's just a mailing list,' she said.

'Is that so?'

'Something like that.'

'I see.'

'So, is that all cleared up to your satisfaction, Mr Plant?'

No, it wasn't. Nor were a lot of things. Most things.

'I'll think about it,' he said, for want of anything better to say. But he would. Brood on it. File it for future reference and brood on it some more, some time. Never come to too sudden a resolution.

Chapter Twenty-one

The prospect of going out on a boat with Murray Brittan filled Plant with trepidation. Trepidation and downright fear. Plant was happy with the idea of boats. He liked to see them on the harbour or Middle Harbour or Pittwater, or anywhere else for that matter, sailing or powering by. Being on one he was less enthusiastic about. The danger, indeed the likelihood, of being hit on the head and knocked overboard. Threshing around there amidst the sharks. He had heard enough about Murray Brittan's reputation. And not just the bottom-of-the-harbour schemes, as they used to call them. There were always highly coloured stories about people like him. Media magnates. Property developers. Financiers. He had no evidence that Murray had ever tossed anybody overboard to the sharks. But he could believe it possible. In principle.

He tried focusing on the motor yacht he had seen moored there. The *Jolly Britannia*. Like a royal yacht taken over by pirates, a republican yacht, privatized now and no doubt working in the tradition of Queen Elizabeth and Drake, piracy with a five hundred percent return on investment. At least it didn't have sails and jibs and booms and the rest of it. All those technical terms. Most of which he didn't know. There was no reason to think he would be flung overboard when the sail swung round since there wasn't a mast or sail. But he couldn't recall whether there were rails round the deck. In his memory it seemed very sleek and sheer and just the sort of thing to slide off. Again the technical terms were beyond the reach of Plant's vocabulary. But an absence of words did not necessarily signify an absence of danger or malign intent.

But when Plant arrived at Murray Brittan's mansion the following morning there had been a change of plan. Or maybe there never had been a plan to go out on the harbour. Maybe that had always been just a form of words. Or a cunning destabilization of Plant's equilibrium and equanimity. Whatever, boating was off the agenda, and they just sat out on the terrace looking at the water, the Harbour Bridge, the seagulls, which was presumably what you did when you had a harbour-side mansion with an expensive water view.

Murray was in casual gear, polo shirt, light tan slacks, moccasins again but without socks this time.

'She stood there,' he said, gesturing. 'Out on the terrace. And she delivered this amazing harangue. A poem, I suppose. It was supposed to be a poetry reading. And she gave this absolutely no-holds-barred attack on all the men she'd known. I thought, this woman is amazing. I've got to have her. So I signed her up. There and then. After she'd finished, needless to say. Not done to interrupt. Though I was tempted, I tell you. So there you have it. What else can I tell you?'

'Why?' Plant asked.

'Why what?'

'Why did you sign her up?'

'Why? Because she had talent. And energy. And chutzpah. And drive. And youth. That was the voice I needed. Enough of the tired old men. I had cupboards full of them. What I needed was the new woman. Someone women readers would respond to. And men would fall for. And she was it. Sheer brilliance.'

He gazed out at the harbour.

'She stood there like a figurehead. Breasting the waves. Surging forward.'

Plant checked out the motor yacht again. It was devoid of any adornment. No bare-breasted goddess of the seas. Just the pointy end of the boat.

'And she signed up?'

'Of course.'

'And then?'

'And then she sailed off.'

'Into the sunset,' Plant offered.

'Into the new dawn.'

'And she became like a roving correspondent.'

'Precisely.'

The water stretched out before them unruffled. Moored boats, moored expensive boats, but no movement. The days when timber freighters and barges and fishing trawlers worked this stretch of the harbour were gone.

'So what is it you are after, Mr Plant?'

'Lambastier's last book. What happened to it?'

'I published it. At least I published the Australian edition. Simultaneously with the American edition. You don't have a copy? You want one?'

'No,' Plant said, 'not that one. I mean yes, I'd like a copy. But it's the unpublished one I'm after.'

'If it wasn't published, then how can I help you?'

'Did you ever see it?'

'Mr Plant, I published her last book. Let me assure you, if there had been another book I would have published it like a shot.'

'So you never had it.'

'Had what, Mr Plant?'

'Her last manuscript.'

'Like I said, any manuscript of hers I would have published.'

He clicked his finger and thumb. 'Like that. Without a moment's hesitation.'

'So you never saw it?'

'Saw what? Something that never existed? How could I?'

'You didn't reject it?'

'Reject it? Liz Lambastier? What a sense of humour you have, Mr Plant. Or unreality. Who would reject such a book?'

'Maybe if the content was, say, troublesome.'

'All the more reason to publish it.'

'Her sister is convinced that there's an unpublished manuscript somewhere.'

'I already told her sister, tell me where and I'll publish it,' Murray said. He snapped his finger and thumb again. 'Like that.'

'But we don't know where, that's what I'm trying to find out. I don't even know if it exists.'

Murray spread his arms and shrugged.

'Then I cannot help you. I would love to publish it. If such a thing exists. But I doubt it, Mr Plant, I very much doubt that it does. No manuscript of Liz Lambastier's would remain unpublished for long.'

'Not with you around, you mean?'

Murray laughed. Two gleaming rows of beautiful teeth. Plant had never gazed into the mouth of a shark but that was what it felt like sitting there.

'Right then,' Plant said.

'Is that all?'

'That's all.'

'I misunderstood. I thought you wanted to talk about Liz. I assumed you were writing about her. A biography, perhaps. So, naturally...'

'I'm sorry,' Plant said. 'No, I'm not writing anything.'

'If I'd known that I could have saved you an unnecessary journey. My apologies, Mr Plant. So, if that's all...'

'I'd be interested in anything you had to say about her. It might help...'

'I'm sure you would,' Murray smiled. 'But I'm sure you're a busy man, like me, so let me let you go.'

He smiled some more.

'And let me assure you, I know nothing of any unpublished manuscript. She never submitted it to me so I doubt very much that it exists. But if it does, rest assured, I should be very interested in publishing it. Obviously. So if it does exist and you find it, Mr Plant, contact me at once.'

It was an order. There was no 'please'.

And that was it.

All very brief. Hardly worth the trouble of having arranged a separate meeting. It could all have been dealt with at the fundraising function. Had Murray expected something more, set aside a space to negotiate?

Chapter Twenty-two

It took a few days for Plant to brace himself to get to the university. It was no longer like the place he remembered. And not just because all the students seemed so much younger than he remembered them. Most of them were evidently recruited from overseas. Now the prime aim of the institution was to make money from foreign students. The whole place emanated the vibes of corporatism and greed. And inflated bureaucracy. Fifty-five per cent of staff were now in administration. Most of the teaching was done by casual, contract staff. Half a million books from the library had been shipped off campus. The vice-chancellor proclaimed the aim of unlearning. True, the grounds had been beautified. Expensively. Not a good sign, prioritising appearances.

But in the end he got himself there. And it was true. Liz had deposited material in the university library. It was listed. In the rare book collection. Plant's idea of rare books was of old bound volumes from the sixteenth or seventeenth century, or even earlier incunabula of the sort Lord Peter Wimsey used to collect. He would never have thought to have looked for an unpublished manuscript there, not a contemporary one. Something from the nineteenth century, perhaps. But why not? Who was to say what was rare? Or what might well become rare? He was still impressed, though, that she had managed to persuade the library into acceptance. A feminist cell in rare books? Maybe a fund for purchasing future feminist rarities. It was odd that she hadn't kept all her papers together in the Mitchell Library. But she wasn't alone among writers in hawking her wares around. Maybe it was about getting the best price at different times. Though wouldn't it be better for your plans for posterity to have all your papers in just one collection? Where fans and researchers and hagiographers could find them easily? Librarians, especially rare book librarians, preferred collections of an author's work to be aggregated into one place. But maybe it was a safety provision, maybe she envisaged a worst-case scenario of the State Library burning down. Or, more likely in present times, the possibility that one of the libraries might decide to purge its holdings and consign whatever was deemed unwanted to remote deposit or landfill.

He filled out the request slip, copying down the call number from the catalogue, and sat at a desk and waited. It was hardly a hive of activity. The days of research into the past looked like they were over. The future was digital, forget fading ink and crumbling paper, illegible handwriting, tired old books. Let the dead bury the dead. And let what wasn't buried be vulnerable to malware, Trojans, cyber attack and the curse of Bill Gates.

The strong, brown cardboard box was delivered to his desk, the old traditional way of storing manuscripts and typescripts and loose papers. He untied the pink tape holding the box together. It was a different world from tapping keyboards and looking at electronic representations on a screen. This was more reminiscent of the early fumblings of sexual experience, trying to undo things, unhitch things, straps, catches, buttons. Or maybe it was that the last time he had fiddled around untying a manuscript box was back in the days when he'd fiddled around trying to gain sexual experience. Or was it that libraries induced these erotic reveries. Again, probably because his initial experience of libraries had coincided with those early yearnings and attempted discoveries, those great hopes and huge desires.

He lifted the lid of the box, took out the four manila folders inside, opened the top one and turned the A4 pages. It was a typescript of one of her travel books, a published one, he recognized the title. A corrected typescript, additions and deletions marked on the pages, in the margins at side, top and bottom. A variant text, no doubt. Or corrected early draft. Rare book material, anyway, for future researchers. He opened the second folder and again it was a revised typescript, different book, again a published one, same sort of annotations and revisions. Same with the third. But the fourth and final folder, similarly a stack of A4 paper, was totally blank. Not even a title page. Or page numbers. Or anything. Just blank sheets, not quite pristine, musty, smelling faintly of cigarette smoke and somewhat yellowed, faded in the way inexpensive typing paper faded over the years.

It would not have been hard to do. Whoever it was could have brought in substitute paper. Maybe they had checked out the typescript earlier, to see how substantial it was, how many pages. And having noted that, they had come in the next time with an equivalent folder of blank paper and at some point when the duty librarian had disappeared to follow up a request, put in the substitute, closed the box, tied the tape and returned it. And then walked out with a folder of typescript, no security device in the binding to set off an alarm at the exit because there was no binding, nothing but loose pages. Why would the person at the checkout imagine these were any other than the work of the person carrying them? It was books they had to make sure of, that they had been duly checked out. With sufficient confidence it would have been easy to have walked out with Lambastier's manuscript. Or typescript. Or print-out. Or whatever it was.

'We can find out who last requested it,' the librarian said. 'Check out the request slip.'

But the name would undoubtedly be false. And the ID presented equally false, not a library borrower's card but some other token that had been presented, but in whatever name undoubtedly false and effectively untraceable. It wasn't that hard to create false ID; and if it was just a matter of handing over a plastic card that wasn't going to be checked out or activated in any way, just held there as a hostage until the requested item was returned, then it was easy enough. Clearly it had been.

'Of course,' Fullalove said, 'there's always the possibility that Lambastier sold a ream of blank paper to the library.'

Of course.

'I think someone might have noticed.'

'You reckon? You've got more confidence in universities and libraries than I have.'

‘I doubt that,’ Plant said. He resented Fullalove’s assumption that everyone but Fullalove was deluded by the system. Every system.

‘There’s still no certainty that your missing manuscript was ever there. This might have been the typescript of one of her published books somebody souvenired.’

‘Pretty unlikely,’ Plant said. ‘Just when we’re looking for the missing one. Pretty amazing coincidence.’

‘Fair enough,’ Fullalove conceded. ‘Though you don’t know when it was pinched. Could have happened ages ago and be nothing to do with your search.’

‘Still pretty unlikely.’

‘Fair enough,’ Fullalove said again. ‘Anyway, I don’t give much for your chances of tracking down whoever did it.’

‘Nor do I.’

‘I guess you could check the paper for fingerprints, but pretty certainly whoever it was would have been onto that and worn gloves. Could have been an inside job for all you know.’

‘Could be.’

‘Could be a mad collector.’

‘Of typescripts? Are there such?’

‘Depends what was in it. Sexual deviance, gossip with blackmail potential, state secrets. Any of that would be enough to motivate someone who was into that stuff. And she’d probably score in all those categories, wouldn’t she?’

‘I’ve no idea.’

‘Why else would anyone have pinched it?’

‘Purely literary values,’ Plant said, a phrase from the past he hadn’t heard or used in a while.

‘I doubt it. Not these days,’ Fullalove said.

‘Probably not,’ Plant agreed.

‘Interesting though,’ Fullalove conceded.

He had insisted that they went out into the appalling heat. So appalling Plant would rather have stayed in Fullalove’s appalling hovel. But Fullalove had needed his coffee fix in air-conditioned chill, so they had trudged along the hot pavements of King Street until Fullalove found a suitable venue. Where they could talk, without surveillance.

'One of your local dives?'

'No way,' Fullalove said. 'You want to tell me your troubles, then you tell me them somewhere where I'm not known. Which includes my house.'

'You're getting worse.'

'Just keeping abreast of the surveillance society. I'm still alive, you may have noticed.'

'And there are people out there trying to kill you.'

'Out here,' Fullalove said, 'forget out there.'

'Are you serious?'

'I hope not. But there's always surveillance. Residence and regular habits are obviously problematic. That's why Bin Laden kept on the move.'

'And look what happened to him.'

'Did I tell you my theory about Bin Laden?' Fullalove asked.

'I'm sure you will if you haven't already.'

'Tell you later. Let's sort out this Lambastier problem. Do you know how she died? Have you thought about that?'

'No, as a matter of fact. Not what I was hired for.'

'You should've. She might've been bumped off to prevent the allegedly missing manuscript from appearing. Alternatively there may be no missing manuscript, merely a red herring to divert attention from the real reason for her murder.'

'We don't know that she was murdered. There's absolutely no reason to think that she was.'

'Of course there is.'

'What?'

'Why else would someone have you look for a missing manuscript?'

'To find it.'

'Why?'

'Well, it's not going to be a first-person account of how I was murdered and who did it to me, is it?'

'There's more to it than just finding it. That's a given. We just need to find out what that more is.'

'We need to do nothing of the sort. I was simply hired to do a thorough library search.'

'The body in the library,' Fullalove intoned. 'Classic scene from the golden age of British murder mysteries. Almost a cliché. Well, definitely a cliché. Your best hope is that this will be a postmodern variant. With no actual body in the library. And no manuscript either. I'd find out how she died if I were you.'

'You reckon?

Fullalove fiddled with a couple of sugar sachets, twisting and bending them in his fingers that would have been happier fiddling with a cigarette or a joint, but the happy days when you could do that in public, and get away with it, were past.

'If someone pinched that manuscript since you started looking for it, that suggests either her sister's place is bugged and they know she's after it, or the state library had the papers flagged, or someone had them flagged, and the alert was triggered as soon as you ordered them up.'

'Is that likely?'

'What else are they going to do all day long with all those monitoring resources they've developed?'

'So someone removed it from the university library just before I got there.'

'Looks like it. Or they could have lifted it ages ago, of course, nothing to do with you looking for it now. Unless it was never there at all. And like I said, she just gave them a stack of blank paper.'

'Unlikely.'

'Unlikely, yes, but you need to consider all the possibilities.'

'So we've considered that possibility. What next?'

'You'd have to ask who could be that organized to pick up on your search and beat you to it. Who'd have the resources? Have to be some special branch or intelligence agency operation. And given that, you'd be advised to backtrack and see what happened to terminate Liz Lambastier's existence.'

'That doesn't necessarily follow.'

'Of course not. But if I were you, and I valued my own continued existence, I'd check it out.'

'Sure. What else?'

'Putting that off, are we? You'd rather find something more appealing while you prevaricate. All right. Next point. How do you know there's only one copy of this missing manuscript? You reckon that was the only copy that exists that got lifted? If it was lifted. Was it typewritten? Maybe there's a carbon copy somewhere. Maybe it was handwritten. There could still be a photocopy. If it was a computer print-out, then there's going to be a copy on someone's computer or old floppy disk or flash drive. Almost certainly.'

'So we hack into everyone's computer? Everyone she ever knew?'

'Probably already been done, if it's serious,' Fullalove said. 'And if it's not serious then we don't need to go to all that trouble and get ourselves into trouble. Stick with the family, just a sisterly inquiry. Not a world pursuit by intelligence agencies and united hackers' mutual society. Not necessarily, anyway. Nonetheless...'

Chapter Twenty-three

Being hit on the head and knocked unconscious was pretty much part of the job description of the traditional private investigator. Despite calling his work research assistance, Plant had not escaped the tradition. He did not appreciate it. A man of non-violence himself, he resented being the recipient of it. Lying on the floor of Claire's apartment he felt, in addition to the pain, considerable annoyance. He must have turned the key and walked in without any care or caution. It had been a mistake, clearly. He opened an eye, cautiously, then the other. Two eyes simply enlarged the view of devastation. The floor was strewn with books, thrown from the shelves, scattered over the full surface of the room. Cushions had been tossed on top of them, chairs and couch stripped and upturned. Cupboard doors hung open in every room. Mattresses stood against walls, sheets, cushions, clothes were scattered and heaped indiscriminately. He must have been struck as soon as he entered the apartment, before he had time to register the chaos. Unless it was still to begin when he arrived. He hadn't seen it, anyway. He hadn't seen anything.

Break-ins always carried their psychic freight. There was the trauma of intrusion, the invasion of one's privacy, the sense that one's own private atmosphere had been penetrated. And the lurking indeterminate smell like the trace of tobacco smoke, some other organism's breath and sweat and physical and psychic exudations that had been deposited and left there lingering. He opened the windows, wide, as wide as he could, to try and disperse the hovering miasma.

He wondered who could have done such a thing. Men of action with a loathing for books, or women of action for that matter? Publishers? University librarians? Literary agents? Young thugs committed to digitization and the internet, wiping out the offensive print culture of the past like USA-funded fundamentalists. Had it been done by a team or just one person? There was no way of telling, no way of telling how long it had taken, how long Plant had lain unconscious.

Presumably whoever it was had been searching for Lambastier's missing manuscript. Unless other apartments in the building had similarly been done over and it was just jewel thieves or some run of the mill attempt at burglary. He did not intend to find out. He was not going to go knocking on other apartment doors. He would leave it to Claire to decide whether to go to the police. He preferred not to himself.

Apart from assuming it was a search for the manuscript he had nothing else to go on. Besides a sore head. That the search had been so thorough or at least so disruptive suggested that someone thought that he or Claire had the manuscript. But that still didn't prove that it existed, or ever had existed. It did suggest that whoever had been searching was concerned to get hold of it. Considerably concerned, and willing to go to some considerable effort to get hold of it. But that still didn't prove that it had ever existed in the first place. Not necessarily.

He found the landline phone amidst the wreckage. It had merely been thrown on the floor, not ripped from its socket. There was still a dial tone. He called Fullalove, gave him the address, asked him to come round and on the way pick up an ice pack at a chemist's to put on his head and limit the bruising.

'Use a packet of frozen peas,' Fullalove suggested.

'I don't have one.'

'Not in the fridge?'

'No.'

'I thought everyone had a bag of frozen peas in the fridge.'

'I don't eat frozen peas. I don't like frozen food.'

'You don't eat them, you keep them for emergencies.'

'Just get me an ice pack, will you.'

'Sure,' Fullalove said. 'Though a packet of peas would probably be cheaper.'

He made a cup of tea and sat down on the couch and had a break. No point in completing the clean-up if he wanted Fullalove's opinion on the devastation and modus operandi.

He wondered about going to a hospital. Emergency. Waiting his turn amongst the heart-attack cases, the overdosed junkies, the bloodstained victims of street and pub brawls, traffic accidents, domestic violence. He knew of people who had died, waiting in Emergency. And how to get there? Phone an ambulance? Get a taxi? Drive? All in all it seemed easier to stay still and do nothing. If he started to feel worse, then he'd go. Get Fullalove to drive him, maybe.

'Some party,' Fullalove remarked, surveying the still chaotic rooms.

'What do you reckon?' Plant asked.

'Someone looking for something?'

'Looks like it.'

'Did they find it?'

'How would I know? Who knows what they were looking for?'

'At a guess I'd say your missing manuscript.'

'Well there's no missing manuscript here now.'

'So did they find it?'

'Who knows? I didn't have it. Obviously someone thought I did or Claire did. But I can't see that she'd hire me to look for it if she already had it. I guess we'll never know.'

'We might.'

'How?'

'If there's another burglary, that will show they didn't get it. Shows they're still looking.'

'So who's going to be burgled next? And how would we know?'

'We'd know if we set a trap. Put the word out that you'd got hold of the manuscript. They'd go for that.'

'And I get hit on the head again? Or killed?'

'Why would they kill you?'

'Because they'd think I'd read it or made a copy of it.'

'But you don't have it.'

'Try telling them that when they break in.'

'It's a risk you'll just have to take.'

'No I don't. I'll make sure everyone knows I don't have it and I've never seen it.'

'Protest too loudly and they'll assume you're lying and break in again.'

'Protest too quietly and I could be dead meat.'

'Could be,' Fullalove agreed, all too readily, undismayed, uninvolved, his attention distracted elsewhere, absorbed in watching the police and military and media helicopters criss-crossing over the city.

'So what do you reckon?' Plant asked.

'Heavy stuff.'

'Yes.'

'Suggests she was into some heavy shit.'

'Who, Lambastier?'

'Who else?'

'Not the sister.'

'Why not?'

Why not indeed? Plant reflected.

'She wouldn't trash her own flat.'

'Why not?'

'Why would she?'

'Depends on what the real story is.'

'I've no idea any more,' Plant said. 'I'd got the impression Lambastier was some fully paid-up feminist. But Angela Dark had no time for her at all.'

'Sounds fair enough,' Fullalove said when Plant had summarized Angela Dark's remarks on Lambastier. Plant had found them fascinating, rifts in a world that he thought still preserved solidarity, even if nothing else did. But to Fullalove there were no surprises.

'Feminism was just a divisive diversion,' he said. 'And a great opportunity for opportunists.'

'A divisive diversion?'

'Exactly. The real aim was to split the progressive forces on the left. They came up with feminism as a way to set women against men and divide the left into two incompatible factions. And it worked. Then they promoted gay lib and multiculturalism and identity politics and that fractured the progressives even further. Great political strategy. The old divide and rule technique of the British Raj.'

'And this "they"?'

'The CIA presumably. Or some related organization or think tank.'

'So you're saying Lambastier was CIA?'

'Could've been. Quite likely. But not necessarily. She might not even have known. Like all those Congress for Cultural Freedom intellectuals who said they never knew the CIA was funding them. Oh what a surprise, how distressing. Ho ho. And I'm not saying she was an actual, literal, on-the-ground spook. Though she might have been. Reporting back on her travels. Cosying-up to all those famous folk you say she swapped birthday cards with. Was that just social climbing or was it more directed? Or she could've just been a courier. You can't trust sensitive stuff to electronic transmission. You can't risk it being intercepted. You can encrypt it but in the end the codes get cracked. So the safest thing is to have couriers carrying the messages. Like Wallis in China in the 1920s. Carrying out missions for United States naval intelligence.'

'Wallis?'

'Wallis Simpson. Duchess of Windsor later. I've got the book if you want to read it. In hardback or paperback. Excellent reading.'

'You've always got the book.'

Fullalove took it as flattery rather than annoyance and smiled agreeably.

'She could've been a spook, she could've been a courier, but I see her more as an agent of influence. That sort of asset. It's a good symbiotic relationship for writers and intelligence agencies. The writers write what the powers that be want to read and the powers that be get them published.

They could rely on her on writing the right thing so they promote her career. Fix her up with fellowships, residencies, internships, publications, awards, prizes. She was just an anodyne force of distraction, someone they could trust not to say anything troublesome.'

'Simple enough.'

'Not really. You've got to find people naturally servile enough to do it – people who want to be writers, or who want the celebrity of writers, but they don't care what they write. They're a special breed. Real writers tend to be more uncooperative, even to have values.'

'And they chose her?'

'Could have. You know how it goes. You just have to get yourself spotted. She could've been spotted at university. Most likely. Or at school, even. Felix Hacker and Murray Brittan might think they discovered her, but she could already have been recruited and pushed in their direction.'

'You're saying she was a spook put onto Murray Brittan or Felix Hacker?'

'No, I'm saying they'd all been recruited by the same outfit, they were all on the books. Doesn't mean she wasn't onto them, of course. They have to keep their tabs on their own. It's a world of total mistrust. They can't finally rely on anyone, pretty obviously. They might have thought they could rely on Lambastier, but they can't be sure. They might have heard about the missing manuscript. Almost certainly they would have. They might be afraid there could be stuff in it they don't want her saying. And they don't want it being published without being vetted first. Which could explain why you got bumped on the head. Don't you reckon?'

'But it was her sister who asked me to find it.'

Fullalove did his just grinning grin.

The ice pack helped but his head was still painfully sore the next day. It took the morning restoring things to some sort of order. Putting the books back on the shelves was simple enough, though someone was going to have to go through them again to restore them to their precise alphabetical order. At least he had not been attacked in Fullalove's hovel he reflected, with a desperate grasp at looking on the bright side. He could have been crushed beneath the sheer weight of books there.

It was something to think about as he began to tidy up the wreckage, fold clothes, put books back in their dust jackets, put the top back on the lavatory cistern, close the door of the freezer, heave the mattresses back onto the bed bases. All good and valuable exercise he told himself as his head throbbed.

Chapter Twenty-four

Fullalove suggested a restorative early dinner. A purgative or cauterizing hot curry. Or a Szechuan Chinese dish. Plant settled for Indian. Hot Madras curry for Fullalove, malai koofta for Plant, pappadums, naan, mango chutney, lime pickle.

'What's she really up to?' Fullalove asked, scattering pappadum fragments around his plate and person in general.

'Who?'

'Your employer. What game is she really playing?'

'I don't know that she's playing any game. She's just trying to find some manuscript that might exist. Or might not.'

'You really believe that?'

'Why not?'

'It's possible. But why would she care?'

'She wants to get it published, presumably.'

'Without seeing it? She doesn't even know whether it's any good or not.'

'Lambastier was a professional. It wouldn't be bad.'

'Maybe.'

Fullalove ripped into the naan, tearing off a strip and stuffing it into his mouth, carrying on talking as he chewed. Plant found it unappealing to watch, but it was the inevitable downside of having Fullalove share his opinions with you over a meal. And satisfyingly fed, Fullalove was always willing to share his theories and speculations. Indeed, try and stop him.

'But you really think that's the reason?'

'What other reason, then?'

'How did Lambastier die?'

'You already asked me that. I've no idea.'

'Don't you think you should find out?'

'Why?'

'What if she was murdered? Was she a junky and someone gave her a hot shot?'

'Who says she was a junky?'

'All those travels in the East. All that bleeding-heart stuff she wrote about AIDS. Those early stories. The company she kept, those pathetic painters and poets who couldn't even do drugs without killing themselves.'

'Who would've given her a hot shot?'

'What about her sister? Maybe they hated each other. Siblings, you know. Family life.'

Fullalove the authority on the dynamics of family life.

'Or maybe one of those agencies she was working for.'

'Press agencies?' Plant asked, sceptically.

Fullalove laughed.

'Yes, press agencies, why not? Good cover. She's got the profile of an intelligence asset. She could've upset someone.'

'Some Islamic fundamentalist she'd been reporting on got wise to her and bumped her off?'

'It would be nice to think so.'

'You really believe that?'

'That she got her comeuppance? Not impossible. Not impossible it was the people she was reporting to.'

'Why?'

'They could have thought she was going rogue. Heard a rumour she was writing an account of her life as a spook so decided to terminate her.'

'And that's why her sister's looking for the manuscript?'

'No, mate. You're the one looking for the manuscript, you're in the firing line, she's made sure of that, you'll be taking the heat if anything happens.'

'Thanks for telling me.'

'You mean you hadn't worked it out for yourself?'

'Why do you think anybody would care about a manuscript that may not even exist, unless they're afraid it's got some hot stuff in it?'

'By hot you mean sex?'

'Could be. Something implicating her sister, maybe.'

'Oh, so Claire's an agent too, now, is she?'

'I don't see any reason why she couldn't be,' Fullalove said. 'And with that in mind, I'd mind my back if I were you. But actually I was thinking of sex.'

'Which you regularly do.'

'Which I regularly do.'

'And?'

'You think you've been hired to look for a lost literary masterpiece.'

'Mistresspiece.'

'Mistresspiece. And you find you're looking for a fuck and tell diary.'

'The art of our times,' Plant said.

'No it isn't. It's just monomaniacal sleaze, and don't let the publishing industry or the cultural studies collaborators tell you anything else. Just tired old titillating sleaze. But don't let me discourage you from working at it.'

'Thank you.'

'You're welcome. After all, it might be quite entertaining, in a disgusting, distasteful sort of way.'

'I note your recommendation.'

'Seal of approval. Salacious, sleazy and scandalous.'

'Right.'

'Sexual scandal. Sexual jealousy. Sexual competition. It's a powerful motive, too.'

'You're losing me. A powerful motive for what?'

'For bumping someone off. For suppressing a manuscript.'

'So now I'm looking to find a manuscript in order for it to be suppressed?'

'Hadn't you thought of that?'

'No, I hadn't.'

Fullalove grinned. The man who thought of everything.

'And I'm not thinking it now, either.'

'Maybe you should. Maybe there's a lot of things you should be thinking of that you haven't been thinking of.'

'No doubt,' Plant agreed.

'Like, is Claire really Lambastier's sister? Did Lambastier have a sister? Have you checked yet?'

'No, I haven't checked,' Plant admitted.

'Why not?'

'I haven't seen any need to.'

'Perhaps you should.'

'It's not my business. I wasn't hired to investigate that.'

'Still, it would be good to know.'

'It might be interesting, but whether it would be good, I don't know. I'm happy just to leave it. Who else would she be if she wasn't her sister?'

'Who indeed? It could be interesting. She could be anyone.'

'So what do I do, ask her?'

'Depends what sort of answer you want.'

Chapter Twenty-five

Plant was about to open the door of the Neutral Bay apartment when he registered something wrong. Something alarming. There were sounds coming from within. Voices. He had no wish to be hit on the head again. At least this time he had been alerted. Pity about the previous time. He held off from inserting the key into the lock, listened more carefully. Could be radio or television. But that still meant that someone was in there, or had been in there. Pretty definitely electronic voices. Pretty definitely. Not a reception committee. Apparently. But nothing is certain in this world. Certainly not in Plant's world. He waited, held his breath. Listened. The voices continued. He waited some more. The lift door down the corridor opened, someone emerged, looked at Plant suspiciously. At least Plant assumed it was suspiciously. He knocked on the apartment door. If armed assailants emerged maybe the person down the corridor would be a witness. Or another victim.

The door opened fractionally, as far as the security chain allowed. Claire peered through.

'Plant! What are you doing? Why are you knocking, don't you have your key?'

The person from the lift went into one of the apartments.

'No, no, I've got the key.'

He brandished it, held it up, wriggled it.

'I thought I heard sounds,' he said.

'You did. Come in.'

'I can't. It won't open.'

She unhooked the security chain. 'Oops, sorry, forgot about that.'

The radio held forth in the background. So she was a radio person. Couldn't stand it himself, all those endless, assertive voices. He wondered if it was a gender thing, listening to radio.

'I flew down as soon as I got your message,' she said.

Clearly. Or maybe she merely meant she'd flown rather than driven. Which was how he had still been able to park in the designated parking bay.

'I thought I'd better check out the damage,' she said.

'There wasn't much actual damage. I sort of put everything back where it belonged. As far as I could tell. Not sure about the books.'

She looked at the shelves.

'Someone must have assumed you had the manuscript hidden here.'

'I wouldn't have needed to hire you if I had it,' she said.

'They mightn't have known that. Or they might have thought I'd picked it up when I went to Agent Orange's.'

'Unless it was just a routine burglary.'

'No sign of any others in the building,' he said. 'There would have been police around.'

'Have you asked?'

'I haven't said anything to anyone.'

Except for Fullalove, but no point in complicating things at this point.

'Not even the police?'

'I left that to you.'

'To me?'

'Reporting it.'

'Is there any point?' she asked.

Plant shrugged.

'They're not going to be very concerned about a missing manuscript.'

'And a blow to the head,' he added.

'Does it still hurt?'

'Sure it still hurts.'

'Did you check with the hospital?'

'I can tell it hurts without going there. No, it'll be fine.'

'I don't see any point in involving the police,' she said.

He wondered why not. Though basically he agreed. But he still wondered why not. She didn't strike him as the sort of person who was uncaring about possessions or intrusion.

'What about the surveillance set up?' he asked.

'Oh that,' she said. 'You noticed. No, it was switched off.'

'Switched off? Why?'

'Courtesy,' she said. 'Politeness. I didn't want to seem to be checking up on you.'

He wasn't sure that he believed her. Believed that it was not switched on, or switched off from politeness. Pity if it was true. It meant that there was no way of identifying his assailant. Or assailants.

'That was nice of you.'

'It's not mine, anyway,' she said.

He felt a rush of spontaneous fear. Whose surveillance system was it if not hers?

'It was already here. It's not actually my flat, I'm sort of sub-letting it.'

'Sort of.'

'Well, you know, sort of house sitting.'

'So whose place is it?'

'Oh, friends, you know, people I know.'

'What sort of people?'

'Just people,' she said.

She obviously wasn't going to be specific. He didn't feel he could push her. But he didn't feel good about it. Not at all. It might explain why there were no copies of any of Lambastier's books in the bookshelves. But it raised a lot of other questions.

'How many people have you told about looking for Liz's manuscript?' he asked.

'Hardly anyone. Why would I?'

'The more people who knew you were after it, the more likely you'd be to find it.'

'I hired you to find it.'

'Someone must have known. They must have been watching me. Or you. They could have been watching you when you met me up in Mullumbimby. Bugged your phone.'

'You think? Who would bug my phone? Why not your phone?'

'Sure,' he said. 'But whichever it was, it had to be someone with high-tech skills. Professionals. Not your average low-life burglar.'

'It doesn't make sense. Why would someone be so keen to get hold of an old manuscript?'

'Why are you?'

She seemed affronted.

'She was my sister.'

'You didn't like her.'

'Who says that?'

'A number of people, actually.'

'Well,' she said, 'sisters, you know, there's always some degree of tension. Competitiveness, you know.'

He didn't know. He said nothing, just looked at her.

'I hired you to look for Liz's manuscript,' she said, 'not to check up on my private life.'

He carried on just looking.

'Do you want a coffee?' she asked.

It wasn't as much of a non sequitur as it might have seemed. More of a, let's sit down over coffee and I'll come clean. Cleanish, anyway.

He didn't want a coffee but he accepted it. They sat at the kitchen bench. He could have suggested running the taps to make it harder to be heard if the whole apartment was bugged. But the radio probably did that sufficiently.

'The thing about Liz was that you couldn't trust her. She had this massive disregard of other people.'

Plant nodded.

'You heard?'

He nodded some more.

'There was no way of knowing what she might have written. She might have put anything down without caring who it hurt. So an unpublished last manuscript of hers could be like a time bomb. If someone came across it they might have found all sorts of stuff.'

'What sort of stuff?'

'Stuff. Who knows?'

'Sex romps along with her sister?'

She flushed.

'No,' she said, 'not at all, absolutely not. I was never mixed up in that.'

'So what are you worried about?'

'I don't know,' she said. 'That's the point, can't you see? I don't know what she might come up with.'

He didn't believe her especially, but he left it at that.

'But you want it found. And then what? Destroyed?'

'No, no. I wouldn't destroy it.'

'Edited, then.'

'No, no, you're missing the point. I don't even know if it exists. I hope it doesn't, really. I just want to be sure it's not ticking away somewhere.'

'You can never be sure something doesn't exist,' Plant said. Philosophic mode. 'You can be sure when something does exist because you can see it or touch it. Look, a book. But even when the evidence suggests something doesn't exist, you can still never be sure that it doesn't exist somewhere.'

'Oh, let's have a drink,' she said.

She brought out a bottle of Hunter Valley red and a couple of glasses from the kitchen. Plant didn't want a drink right now any more than he'd wanted the coffee. A gentle blast of marijuana heads was what he wanted. But he accepted the glass she poured, raised it with a 'Cheers', and took a careful sip. He was no connoisseur but it seemed all right.

'That's better,' she said, taking a swig, followed by a second one.

'Do you think anyone actually read her books?' she asked. 'I mean, people obviously bought them. Or some people did. They bought them to give as presents. Or to read about somewhere you might want to go on your next holiday. She'd got herself a name, people recognized it. But did anyone actually read the books? From cover to cover?'

'They'd need to sell in pretty large numbers to sustain her lifestyle. Travelling round the world. Hotels and airlines don't come cheap.'

'That's why she wrote for the magazines. They used to pay well.'

'You think someone could have recruited her for secret service work?' Plant said, floating Fullalove's suggestion. 'She was a writer, a traveller. Classic profile.'

'Why wouldn't they?' she said.

'And she'd have been up for it?'

'Why not? Anything devious, dodgy, downright dishonest and treacherous would be right up her alley. She wouldn't be able to resist.'

She poured herself another glass.

'Help yourself,' she said to Plant.

'Thanks,' he said. But he was still sipping slowly at his first.

'And sex?' Plant asked. Perhaps too eagerly.

She looked at him suspiciously. 'What do you mean?'

'Could there be some sex stuff in the manuscript that someone mightn't want published.'

'Getting excited about it, are you? Down, Bonzo, down.'

'Bonzo?'

'Yes, you,' she said. 'You were probably as bad as she was.'

'Bad?'

'Promiscuous. She certainly spread it around. Like you, I imagine. You'd have fucked her, Plant. In fact maybe you did. Did you? Why haven't you told me?'

'I think I would have been too young.'

'That wouldn't have stopped her. She liked them young.'

'No, I never did.'

'Are you sure?'

'I think I'd remember.'

'That's not a straight answer.'

'I never even met her.'

'You're still not answering the question.'

'You think I had remote sex with her? Like without actually meeting her?'

'You tell me.'

'No, then. The answer is no.'

'See,' she said. 'That wasn't that hard, was it?'

Claire was hoeing into the wine. Plant occasionally poured a drop into his own glass to give the impression he was keeping up with her. But he was only taking the odd sip. With the bottle nearly emptied, he popped the question. 'You don't actually know that the manuscript exists, do you?'

'She was always writing.'

'Maybe. Did you ever see any of it?'

'She wouldn't just have stopped. She always wrote up what she'd been doing, that was the only reason she did anything, to write about. And there hadn't been a new book for a while. Not published. So...'

'So you think she must have been writing one yet to be published.'

'Yes.'

He tried playing it tough. Private-eye tough, glass in hand.

'There never was a missing manuscript, was there?'

She seemed unfazed, comfortably mellow.

'There might have been.'

'Might have been,' Plant said, dismissively.

'Well, there might have been. It might have explained what happened to her.'

'What did happen to her?'

'That's what I don't know.'

'And the answer lies in a missing manuscript that probably never existed in the first place.'

'Maybe.'

'And you think this hypothetical work will provide the answers you want.'

'Yes.'

'Even if it never existed, its absence will tell you something?'

'It might,' she said. 'It might give a lead to how she died.'

'Is there a question about that?'

She looked doubtful.

'I don't know. What do you think?'

'I don't know. You tell me.'

'I don't know either. That's why I need to find out what happened. I'm serious,' she said. 'I think something's not right.'

'And you want to know what.'

She nodded. 'Yes.'

'You want me to find out how she died? Is that what all this is about?'

Was she serious? Or was this just a bit of self-dramatizing, fuelled by most of the bottle of wine. Was she emotional, excessive? Or straightforward, clear-headed? He didn't know. He had no idea what he was in for. If anything. But it tied in with the questions Fullalove had been raising about how Lambastier had died.

'Now you tell me,' Plant said, somewhat unchivalrously.

'So what did Liz die of?' Plant asked.

'Natural causes.'

'Like what?'

'I've no idea. I wasn't there.'

'Like heart attack, liver failure?'

'I don't know.'

'You're sure it was natural causes.'

'Why wouldn't it be?'

'Where's she buried?'

'She was cremated.'

'So no exhumation.'

'Oh really,' Claire said.

'I had to ask.'

'Why?'

Why? Because Fullalove had planted the germ of suspicion. He just wanted assurance.

Claire offered it.

'Of course it was natural causes. I'm just being silly.'

'Fine,' he said.

If only it was. If only he could leave it at that.

He tracked down the obituaries of Lambastier. None of them specified the cause of death. Sometimes obituaries did, sometimes they didn't. It was not necessarily significant that they hadn't been specific with Lambastier, nor that they hadn't just said natural causes. Nor was it necessarily significant that none of them had mentioned that she was survived by any siblings.

Chapter Twenty-six

Plant phoned Fullalove.

'Is it all right to move into your place for a few days?'

'A few days being how long?'

'As long as it takes. Couple of weeks at most.'

'Couple of weeks?'

'Maybe three.'

'Sure. No problem.'

People seemed not to be a problem for Fullalove. He seemed to have little to do with them generally, preferring a smoke and a book and a conspiracy theory. But he had no problem about dealing with them, even having Plant stay. If people were around he could try out his ideas on them, assuming they had passed his stringent suspicion tests, that they were safe to talk to; if they weren't there or hadn't passed the test, he just examined the thought himself, silently. It was a world of thought forms amidst the stacks of books covering the walls and much of the floor. It was chaotic and dust-ridden and the kitchen approached the squalid. And yet it felt more comfortable and relaxed, more familiar than the order of Claire's Neutral Bay apartment. Or whoever's apartment it was. The comfortable might border on the unhygienic, but sometimes that was easier to take than the order merging into sterility. And he could have a smoke at Fullalove's without any need for precautions and concealment and subterfuge, two or three smokes in succession if he needed, and sometimes he did need, or wanted, and why deny wants, better satisfy them than develop an insatiable need, which he probably had anyway, if he thought about it. He thought about it a bit, the ideas flowed, his body relaxed, it was all a lot more satisfactory.

And he was no longer sure about Claire's apartment, not after being hit on the head. Was it bugged? Was it actively surveilled? Had he been followed? Had someone known he was there or had they expected it to be unoccupied? He felt more at ease at Fullalove's, with the inner-city window-bars and the triple door-locks and the rest of the precautions. Fullalove may have been obsessional, indeed he undoubtedly was, but the obsessions and disorder had a familiarity that was acceptable, reassuring, cosy. It made Plant feel safer, anyway. It had been all too convenient having Claire's apartment provided for him, at his disposal. Had he been getting too staid, rejecting Fullalove's squalor, and walking into a trap? Probably, he decided. Too late now to worry about it.

Claire had protested that there was no need for him to go. Absolutely not. Feel free to stay. But he didn't feel free there. Not now she had arrived. Nor did he want to feel too free. Her heart wasn't in it, he could tell. Nor her body. She had no wish to encourage intimacy. It was something of a relief. Intimacy with clients or suspects was not a good idea. And no point in telling himself he wasn't interested. He wasn't. But that didn't stop situations from developing, situations which were equally fraught whether they involved backing off or giving in. Giving in sounded a bit weak. Going ahead, then. Plunging in. Maybe. Either way it was all fraught. The proximity. The potential for opening the wrong door at the wrong time, making the wrong aside, the wrong compliment, the inappropriate remark. And all that. At least Fullalove wouldn't be a problem in that area. The streets of Newtown had never seemed quite so welcoming.

'What about Murray's empire going down, according to Hacker?'

'No great loss,' Fullalove said. 'Not in itself. All old media's going down. An entire culture is being wiped out. Even as we speak. And everyone just accepts it. Murray's no great loss in himself. But print media in general? I dunno, was it ever that good?'

'You'd heard?'

Fullalove shrugged. Although the eager disseminator of evidences of the decline of the west and the end of civilization as we know it, he was never happy to acknowledge other people's similar predictions. Prophets evidently preferred to be lone voices. They liked their isolation. Despised and rejected of men. The last thing they wanted was a ranked chorus of Jeremiads. Even a duet was one too many.

'Depends how much he's diversified,' Fullalove said. 'And who's been actually funding the publishing part of his business. It wouldn't have been his own money so it probably makes no difference.'

Plant offered no comment. He was working at resisting the temptation always to say negative things. True as they might have been. But Fullalove had no such inhibitions.

'It's always good to see these fuckers go down. Except they rarely do. Not fully and completely and totally. Pity though, don't you think?'

'Don't I think what?'

'That it's a pity that these guys don't really go down. Or get strung up for economic crimes against humanity and the dissemination of lies.'

'Strung up? You into capital punishment now?'

'For these fuckers? Too good for them. Put them in the stocks for six months. Reintroduce the pillory. Let them go painfully bust and then make them painfully pay for it and their other crimes.'

'Why not?' Plant found himself saying.

'Except the law never catches up with them. But capitalism does, isn't that neat? The inexorable greed of capitalism to devour its own brings them down. The internet is wiping the floor with them. One greedy pack of liars and tax-evaders destroying an earlier pack. I like it. It you wait around long enough you see justice being done. The evil destroy the evil.'

'But evil still remains,' Plant pointed out.

'That's where the Cathars come in,' Fullalove said. 'They figured the creation was the work of evil.'

'How does that help things?'

'There isn't any help.'

'What's happened to your belief in the inevitable triumph of communism?'

'You're still got to believe it even if you're not sure whether you do any more. It's like Christianity and the nineteenth-century crisis of faith.'

'You're experiencing a crisis of faith?'

'In the world as we see it,' Fullalove said, 'it's hard not to.'

'And hearing that Murray Brittan's going down doesn't cheer you up?'

'That could just be Felix Hacker feeling spiteful now Murray's closed down the magazine he used to edit. Still, better than hearing that Brittan alone of the old media is doing well. So, yeah, notionally cheering.'

'What about magazines?'

'What about them?'

'If their day is over, shouldn't you be collecting them?'

There was a silence as Fullalove considered the proposition.

'If their day is over, what would I be collecting?' he asked eventually.

'Back issues.'

Fullalove considered some more.

'Not sure that there's a great market for back issues of most magazines.'

'Maybe not.'

'They'd create a storage problem,' he said, looking round the room, enclosed in books.

'There already is a storage problem,' Plant pointed out. The list of the politically incorrect and the socially unacceptable grew day by day. Even with the self-storage facility that Fullalove had hired the books were still piling into the house.

Chapter Twenty-seven

Plant lay in bed. Nursing his wounds, as the phrase had it. Except that while the wounds were undoubtedly there, no obvious nursing was being done. It was just a matter of day-by-day letting the sore bits get less sore.

His phone rang.

'Yes,' he snarled, picking up.

'Plant?'

'Who wants to know?'

'Oh, aren't we like a bear with a sore head today. You had a night on the tiles and fell off the roof?'

It was a female person's voice, loud and offensively cheerful. And familiar. Except that he couldn't place it. Maybe he had suffered brain damage and memory loss from blunt force trauma or whatever it was they called it when you were hit on the back of the head. He wasn't sure that he could remember the precise wording. Brain damage certainly a possibility. He groaned with pity for himself.

'Sasha,' Sasha boomed in his ear.

He groaned some more.

'And a nice morning to you, too,' she answered.

'Whadyawant?' Plant asked.

She laughed. Loudly. Too loudly.

What she wanted was that they should meet. She suggested Bondi. She was house sitting there. Well, apartment sitting. Amazing how people landed these amazing houses and apartments, Plant reflected. How come he never had such connections, such contacts? Well, Neutral Bay, perhaps, that had been pretty good. Except for getting hit on the head. But it had nothing like Sasha's view across the beach and out into the ocean. The bright blue of the sky and sea, the glistening sunlight, the general vision of all being well with the world. Bondi itself looked strangely European, Baltic or Black Sea or something, all those buildings rising up from the esplanade, squat, solid. It was always unexpected, contrasting with the open expanse of the stretching sea, tropical, subtropical, whatever, blue and foam-crested and altogether amazing. They sat at the wide picture window, looking down on the far from empty beach.

'How much would Lambastier's manuscript be worth?' Sasha asked.

'Not a lot.'

'That Luke character said a couple of hundred thousand.'

'Luke's thinking about fine art. It's a different world.'

'Don't people collect manuscripts?'

'Probably not like they used to.'

'But it must be worth something.'

'Not necessarily.'

'What would Claire pay for it?'

'No idea. I think she was hoping it would turn up in some library. She wasn't figuring on buying it off someone.'

'But would she? Buy it?'

'You'd have to ask her. It depends if it's any good, I imagine.'

'If it's any good?'

'If it's worth publishing. If it's not worth publishing why would she want to buy it?'

'Sentimental value,' Sasha offered.

'Yeah, well.'

'What about if there's stuff in it?'

'What sort of stuff?'

'Oh, you know.'

Plant didn't. Not specifically. Discreditable stuff, maybe, that Claire might want to suppress. Defamatory stuff that she wouldn't want to risk publishing. Full-on scandalous stuff, was that a possibility? Stuff that she featured in herself, maybe?

'Tell me,' he said.

'Your Claire,' Sasha began.

'She's not my Claire.'

'Your employer, then. Is that it?'

'That's it.'

'Your employer contacted Murray Brittan.'

Plant waited for her to go on.

'Fair enough,' he said.

'She asked him if he had an unpublished book of Lambastier's.'

'And he said no.'

'How did you know that?' Sasha asked.

'He told me.'

'Told you?'

'Well, he didn't tell me that she'd contacted him. But he told me that he told her that he didn't have anything. If he had he would have published it. Or so he said.'

'Maybe not.'

'What do you mean?'

'Well, it depends what it was about, doesn't it?'

'Does it?'

'Whether he would publish it or not.'

'Depends whether it's any good, presumably,' Plant said.

'Or what's in it.'

'What does that mean?'

'There might be things in it someone mightn't want published.'

'What sort of things?'

'Things,' she said.

'Go on.'

'Just things.'

'So though no one's seen this manuscript there might be things in it someone doesn't want published. Even if no one knows whether it even exists or not. Let alone what the things might be.'

'Something like that,' she said.

'And where do you come into this?'

There was a delay before she replied. Always a possibility with a direct question. Plant waited.

'Murray phoned Hilly. He knew Hilly and Lambastier were friends. And he thought that if anyone might know of anything, it might be her.'

'And?'

'So she put him onto me.'

'Why?'

'Because she's getting on and she isn't that mobile and basically she couldn't be fucked.'

'But you could be.'

'Of course. Always.'

She gave him one of those firm, hard, unflinching looks into the eye.

'And?'

'And I've been looking.'

'And?'

'We've found something.'

'Like what?'

'Like a missing manuscript.'

'Really?'

'Well, sort of. Bits of one.'

'Go on,' he said.

'What happened was Lambastier gave Hilly a copy of the original typescript of her first book. You know, the book of stories, the one she dedicated to Hilly.'

'And?'

'The way she'd written it. Before it got edited and bits got chopped out.'

'So you've found a variant text of her first book.'

'It's more than just that,' Sasha said. 'There were whole stories left out.'

'Why? Because they weren't up to scratch?'

'No. Nothing like that. Because they were too hot to handle.'

'Oh yes?'

'Seriously.'

'Too hot for who?'

'Murray, basically. He was the publisher. And he made sure some stuff was left out.'

'What sort of stuff?'

'About Murray, of course. The Beast of Birchgrove. The Sexual Sleaze of Snail's Bay. The Lecher of Long Nose Point.'

'Really?'

'You better believe it.'

'I can believe it.'

'Exactly.'

'What do you mean, exactly?'

'Other people are going to believe it, too. If that stuff ever gets out, it'll generate a tsunami of allegations. More stuff will come out. The internet will be full of it. There's going to be a queue of people lining up to tell their tales of how Murray sexually monstered them and harassed them and all the rest of it. In this climate he'd be fucked. And not in the way he used to like to be. Millions in compensation claims. His name would be trashed. He'd be ruined.'

'So has Murray seen this stuff?'

'Of course he's seen it. That's why it was cut out in the first place.'

'That was years ago.'

'He doesn't forget stuff like that.'

'So he wants to suppress it.'

'Well, he's not going to want to see it published, obviously.'

'Because it makes him look bad.'

'He never worried about looking bad. But things have changed. He doesn't want a whole lot of women coming forward and saying what he did to them.'

'What did he do to them?'

'He's not going to have told me,' Sasha said.

'I suppose not. Unless...'

'Forget it,' she said. 'No way he's into self-incrimination.'

'Nor you, I guess,' Plant hazarded a guess.

She ignored it.

'Look,' she said, 'the reality is Murray can't remember half of what he might have done. And what he does remember he prefers to forget, it was a long time ago, it deserves to be forgotten. That's his story, anyway.'

'So the bits cut out of her book...'

'There's stuff in them that's clearly about Murray. Everyone knows she started off writing for his magazine. There's a piece she called "Fucking my way into journalism." How about that for a title? And it's transparent. Big-shot magazine owner, "You wanna job so give me a blow job, good, now how about a fuck, you don't need to smile, just open your fucking legs or I will." That sort of stuff. I'm quoting from memory but it captures Murray's idiom, don't you think? Immediately recognizable, wouldn't you say? And if that ever got published there would be hordes of women crawling out of the woodwork saying "The same thing happened to me."'

'So Lambastier was doing a job on him.'

'Yes and no.'

'Yes and no?'

'She was cool about it, according to Hilly. She just told it like it was. No big deal. A girl's got to do what a girl's got to do. To get published. To get ahead. So she wasn't too worried about it. She could give as good as she got when it came down to it. But other women were like more delicate, more sensitive, more innocent, so it used to come as a shock to them.'

'But no one ever said anything.'

'Depends who you listen to. Everyone in the business knew what he was like. But that was the nature of the business. Like the movies. Like television. Like politics. Like royalty.'

'Royalty?' Plant asked. 'You've got intimate knowledge of bad behaviour at the palace?'

She smiled. Grinned.

'So everyone knew about Murray but no one's complained.'

'They settled out of court.'

'Who?'

'Women who complained. All hushed up with big payments and confidentiality agreements.'

'So nothing will come out.'

'There's lots more.'

'More people or more stuff?'

'Both.'

'And he doesn't want to pay out any more, is that it? Is he broke, or something? I guess he could be if the company's going down.'

'It's not just a matter of paying out. It doesn't work like that these days. In the current climate they'll all go public and there'll be a full-on trial by media. Old media, social media, the lot. A total witch-hunt. Before they ever get around to talking money. Or going to court. They've kept the lid on it for years but times have changed. So the last thing he wants is Lambastier stirring stuff up from the grave and giving people ideas of going public now.'

'And you're saying that in the bits that got left out she was doing an exposé of Murray.'

'It was a story. She was using it. Like the harassment. Which she used for her career. So she wasn't exactly exposing it. Just telling it like it was. She was quite happy to go along with it. People did. It was the way to get ahead. If you didn't like it, fair enough, go get another job. But no one did. Because there weren't any other jobs as good. So you let the boss grope you or bonk you or jerk off in front of you, and you soared ahead.'

'But she cut all this out of the book.'

'Some of it, anyway. Murray obviously said he'd publish it. But leave some of it out. So she went along with that in order to get published like people do. Like she'd gone along with the rest of it.'

'And she never reprinted the cuts anywhere?'

'I guess she decided they didn't exactly add to her credibility or her feminist image. So it suited her like it suited Murray just to leave all that alone. So the book was never reprinted, not even with the cut stuff still left out.'

'And now you want to restore the missing bits and reprint.'

'Not me,' Sasha said.

'Nor Murray, presumably.'

'No, just your Claire.'

'She's not my Claire and I've no reason to think she wants the stuff reprinted.'

'Then why's she got you to look for it?'

'Same reason as Murray got you, presumably,' he said. 'To make sure it all stays unpublished, I imagine.'

'So basically we've just been wasting our time, both of us, looking for something no one wants published.'

'Pretty much,' Plant agreed.

'So there's still no missing manuscript as such. Just the leftovers from her first book.'

'There's quite a lot of that. It would've made a full-length book if they'd left it all in.'

As it was it had come to a brief hundred and twenty-eight pages, he recalled. So say some sixty or more pages excised. Not exactly a missing manuscript.

'Claire was sure Liz would have written a memoir. How could a narcissist like that not have?'

'Easy,' Sasha said. 'Assemble a massive deposit of your papers and correspondence and the rest of it and foist it on some library as bait and wait for someone else to write it.'

'Could be,' Plant agreed.

'You haven't found anything. You got a better theory?'

'No.'

'Well, that's my bet. There isn't anything else.'

'Seems not.'

'But what we've got is quite enough.'

'Quite enough for what?'

'For Murray and Claire to deal with.'

'And how are they going to do that?'

'I guess we'll have to wait and see,' she said.

'Have you read it?' Plant asked.

'Of course.'

'What's it like?'

She laughed.

'Depends what you have in mind. It's well enough written. No problem there.'

'So what's the problem?'

'It depends what your employer wants.'

'Is it publishable?'

'Is that what she wants? I doubt she does somehow, not this stuff.'

'What else?'

'Maybe what's actually said.'

'Like what?'

'Like the content.'

'What about it?'

'Use it to expose Murray.'

'Why would she do that?'

'That's what he's worried about. Why else would she be looking for it?'

Was that what Claire had in mind? Plant wondered. He hadn't thought of that until now. Was she out to expose Murray from some position of outrage, feminist, sisterly, human decency? And even if Lambastier wasn't going to be pressing harassment charges from the grave, other people would if they got to read the material. And according to Sasha's account of Murray's fears, there clearly were other people, and no shortage of them.

Plant looked at the view, the stretching ocean, the arching sky. Surfers drifted amongst the waves, sunbathers clustered on the beach.

'So what's the deal?' he asked.

'Deal?'

'Deal,' he said. 'You want Claire to cough up and buy it? You running an auction? With Murray and Claire bidding against each other?'

'I'm just letting you know the state of play.'

'State of play?'

It sounded oddly athletic. Maybe it went along with that gym-gear fitness-freak style.

'How things are.'

'So how are they?' he asked. 'You've found a chunk of unpublished material. Not exactly a missing manuscript. But close, maybe. Where do we go from here?'

'You were the one hired to look for it. Where do you want to go?'

'Are you offering it to Claire? Or have you already done a deal with Murray?'

'I haven't done any deal.'

'So where is it?'

'Safe,' she said.

'And you want to sell it?'

'I think we need to set up a meeting between Murray and Claire,' she said.

'Is that what he wants?'

'You got a better idea?' she asked.

Sasha produced a joint from a silver cigarette case, rolled and ready to go. Forward planning. None of the scrabbling around looking for papers, looking for dope, rolling it as the need arose. It was the sort of detail that ought to be usable in some instant character analysis, Plant reflected.

She lit it, drew on it, handed it across to Plant and smiled. It was the smile that was the problem. She'd done it before. Was he so unused to smiles? Or was it because they could mean so many and contradictory things? Here, share this smoke. Here, sucker, who knows what this is laced with. Got you now, mate, I've got the manuscript and you don't know what to do next. Or maybe, even, hey let's relax, have a smoke, lovely day, what do you want to do for the rest of it, have some fun? But he couldn't read the signals. The context all inviting and pleasurable enough but you never knew any more. Murray Brittan's anxieties were surely warning enough. He tried a tentative smile back. She winked.

'You want a coffee or something?'

He settled for coffee.

He considered asking, was it you who broke into Claire's and hit me on the head? But that could produce as disastrous a reaction as making an expression of sexual interest. Like another sharp blow to the head from some handy kitchen instrument, rolling pin or meat tenderizer. And he had no reason to ask it, beyond suspicion. That lingering smell of tobacco. Like the tobacco she mixed in with the dope.

All in all it seemed better, safer, just to gaze out of the window at the beach and the bodies lying on it and generally disporting themselves.

'Here you are,' she said, handing him his coffee.

He thanked her, smiled. Maybe he was looking friendly, forgiving.

'I didn't mean to hurt you the other night,' she said. 'I just hit you without thinking. I didn't know it was you. At your apartment,' she added, in case he wasn't sure what she meant.

'Who did you think it was if it wasn't me?'

'I didn't think,' she said. 'I just reacted automatically and took a swipe.'

She made it sound like opening a hotel door with a swipe card.

'Because if I'd thought it was you I wouldn't have been able to do it and then you would have seen it was me breaking in and then we would have been fucked.'

'We?'

'Well, me, then.'

'And now we're not?'

'I'm sorry,' she said. 'It's just part of the job.'

He considered that.

'Sure, what's a blow to the back of the head amongst friends?'

She reached out a hand and touched him on the forearm.

'I'm glad that you see it like that,' she said. 'Thank you.'

He wasn't sure that he did see it like that, but what the hell?

'So why did you break in?'

'I wasn't sure whether you'd found anything. I mean, I didn't know whether there actually was another book, not just the stuff Hilly had, and you'd managed to get hold of it somehow.'

'You could have asked,' he said.

'I guess I didn't think of that. Sorry.'

It was all very cosy and friendly. Even approaching the intimate. The touch of her hand on his arm. He touched the back of his head with his free hand to remind himself of that previous physical encounter. Conflicted, was that how he felt? Maybe safest just to stay that way.

Chapter Twenty-eight

An evening cruise on the harbour in the *Jolly Britannia* was not something that filled Plant with elation or excitement or enthusiasm. It came into the category of unappealing. But more and more things had become unappealing, over the years, in the light of experience. And unappealing was only a part of it in this case. There was also suspicion and trepidation and indeed downright fear. Not something to look forward to.

But Claire had insisted.

'I might need you.'

Just might need him. Not even a certainty. He tried wriggling out of it. But she was adamant.

'A witness,' she said, when he asked what she might need him for.

'A witness of what?'

'Whatever agreement Murray or Sasha comes up with.'

'That sort of witness.'

'What did you think I meant?'

He shook his head. Nothing. Just a witness to observe mayhem or murder or theft or destruction. Though maybe she had it right. It was just going to be a matter of witnessing a signature to whatever deal was agreed on. Signed on board a yacht or whatever Murray called it. Boat. Ship. How civilized. He wished he could believe it.

'Why does it have to be a meeting on his boat?'

'It's a celebration.'

'Celebrating what?'

'An agreement.'

'Agreeing to what?'

'Whatever we agree to,' she said.

'Which is what?'

'How will I know till I get there?'

'Are you sure you know what you're doing?'

She looked put out at that. She gave a chill 'Yes'.

'I don't see why it has to be done on board a boat.'

'That's the way Murray does things.'

'Really? He thinks he's an admiral or something? And we have to go along with it?'

'What's the problem? A harbour cruise, it could be fun.'

'Fun?' he said. 'It could be a nightmare.'

'Don't be so negative.'

He couldn't see any reason not to be. But it had clearly already been decided.

'Wear a lifejacket,' Fullalove said.

'A lifejacket? I don't have one, why would I?'

'To save your life. Go and get one.'

'How can I turn up on board in a lifejacket?'

'Easily. Safe sailing.'

'It would look like I don't trust Murray. Or any of them. And not just in the mere matter of seamanship.'

'Well you don't, do you? You'd be mad to trust any of them. Murray, Claire, Sasha... Any one of them could give you a push over the side.'

'Thanks for the thought. Why would they do that?'

'To get rid of you. The man who knew too much.'

'I'm not sure I know anything.'

'But they don't know that, do they? They might think you've got it all worked out.'

'Got what all worked out?'

'Who knows? You don't have to say anything. Best you say nothing so they don't take a swipe at you. Just wear your lifejacket.'

'I don't have one, I told you.'

'Then I'd get one, pretty quick smart.'

'How can I wear it?'

'Under a shirt. Or a windcheater. It'll just look like you've put on a bit of weight. Or you feel the cold so you've put a padded jacket on. No problem.'

'I'd look ridiculous.'

'So what? In that company who'd notice?'

'Everyone.'

'So get one of those they have on aircraft. Inflate it when you hit the water and then blow the whistle to attract attention. As long as you haven't been hit on the head and knocked out first.'

'You're a bundle of joy, Fullalove.'

'That's me,' Fullalove agreed. 'That's my name, that's my nature.'

Chapter Twenty-nine

There were always stories in Sydney about boats like the *Jolly Britannia*. Boats in general. The floating gambling games, poker and blackjack and whatever else, high rollers rolling with the waves. Or the floating brothel, one gigantic waterbed rocking and rolling. Or out through the Heads, then the rendezvous with a freighter, pick up a consignment of cocaine or heroin or amphetamines tossed overboard and floating there with a homing beacon.

Sasha was waiting at Murray's when Claire and Plant arrived in Balmain. She was wearing some superwoman space creature outfit, all clinging silver Lycra and a backpack that might have housed a rotor blade for her to buzz around the sky with.

'Come through,' she said.

She took them down to the jetty and gave a call on her phone. A dinghy chugged in from the *Jolly Britannia* and picked them up, driven by someone in nautical uniform, white shirt, white trousers. At least that suggested they were not going to be at the mercy of Murray's seamanship. Not that Plant knew anything about Murray's seamanship, whether it was skilled or non-existent: but he felt a lot safer at the possibility of a professional in charge. Even if Murray chose to demonstrate his own skills once in a while. Plant assumed that he probably would. That sort of person.

Murray was already on board, talking to Felix and Ghostly. He was doing the full-on casual number, overdoing it somewhat, black T-shirt, black shorts and barefooted, not exactly old ram dressed as lamb, maybe just fit, flexing his biceps there, a deep suntan, swarthy even. Felix was the same as ever, crumpled off-the-peg grey suit, scuffed black shoes, and bow tie slightly askew, like some displaced flâneur, some belated boulevardier, a glimpse of archival footage of Old Europe. Ghostly was the same as usual too, his navy blue blazer not an attempt to present a nautical note but the way he always dressed, the way he had dressed at school and had seen no need to change from, unpressed grey trousers, crumpled white shirt, tie knotted but loose at the neck. Like a noose, Plant reflected. No one seemed to be wearing lifejackets. Not even Plant.

'Your choice,' Fullalove had said. 'Don't say I didn't warn you.'

They stood on the deck a while, looking at the night around them. There were lights in the houses bordering the harbour, lights on the Harbour Bridge, but the harbour itself was dark, no moon illuminating anything, no stars to be seen, heavy cloud cover.

The motor started up and the anchor was weighed and they headed off into the night. Murray shepherded them down the stairs into the saloon and offered them drinks. Ghostly and Felix went for the spirits, Claire and Sasha for white wine. Murray poured himself a mineral water. Plant did the same. The sort of occasion when you might need your wits about you.

There was an array of food to pick at. Not just meaty things, but falafel, stuffed vine leaves, olives, hummus, baba ghannouj, tabouli, unleavened bread. Ghostly and Felix got stuck into it. Claire and Sasha made the occasional foray. Murray beamed at them but ate nothing himself. Plant began by following Murray's example but soon moved to an occasional foray and finally joined Ghostly and Felix in piling a selection of items onto a plate. They welcomed him into their company, always glad to attract an audience, silently gesturing to a seat beside them, as they continued their uninterrupted discussion of the state of state politics and the state of the media. Plant listened on the principle that though you might not be at all interested in the topics, nevertheless some scraps of useful information might be picked up. At the gossip level. The discreditable, preferably. And Ghostly and Felix were professionals in the gossip trade. They not only seemed to know all the dirt, or at least a lot of it, but they had also been around long enough to connect the dots, to see the patterns, to make the imaginative leaps that connected the unsuspected to each other. It was like an eighteenth-century coffee house, the way they exchanged rumour and embroidered on speculation. The last days of the old media. As they kept reminding each other. We were lucky to have known it, they told each other. And now they could tell each other all the old stories they each knew by heart, but with Plant there providing the excuse for repeating them.

At some point Sasha had dug out a packet of cigarettes from her backpack and Murray suggested they went up onto the deck. Suggested politely but with that steely focus that produced its desired results with such seeming effortlessness. They went up on deck, Sasha, Murray, and Claire. Plant noticed them leave. They didn't suggest he join them. None of them. But Ghostly and Felix were diverting enough to exclude any anxiety that Claire and Sasha and Murray were excluding him.

'Remember the old *Bulletin*, when Sir Frank used to do a blitz and order everyone's by-line down to ten point?' Ghostly recalled.

'Eight point,' Felix said.

'I was never reduced that low.'

'And then over time they gradually crept back up again to fourteen point, but you probably never got that high, either, did you?'

'What about the time the television critic's copy was thrown out of the window?'

'In the days when windows opened.'

'When he said it was hard coming up with a good column every week, the editor tossed it out and said "Just give us the good ones."'

'And the way the arts editor or the books editor or whoever was dealing with the poems had to read every poem for obscene acrostics after someone had slipped one in.'

'"Fuck all editors,"' Ghostly recalled, with some satisfaction, never having been an editor himself.

'And remember the safe at *Truth*. Where the hot stories were locked away.'

Did they really go back that far, were these personal recollections, or were they folk memories, the cultural myths of a dying culture?

Spirits poured, spirits consumed, spirits raised. Stories for the sake of stories, not necessarily pertinent to anything. But who knew what was pertinent until it turned out to be?

Ghostly was onto the old Journalists' Club. 'Remember Kenneth Slessor tossing salads. Our poet of the city become journalist and editor. And Inky Stevenson dropping down dead at the dinner table.'

'Was it the dinner table?' Felix asked. 'I thought it was in the street.'

'Wasn't that Guy Howarth? The bloke who started *Southerly*. Mugged at Town Hall station and staggered out into the street and got run over.'

Sitting down in the saloon, listening to Ghostly and Felix reminiscing about days of yore, Plant had no idea where they were on the harbour, whether they'd passed beneath the bridge and were headed for the Heads, or had turned in the other direction up the Parramatta River. They could have been anywhere. Wherever they were, there was nothing to be seen through the portholes but darkness.

And then there was a shout up on deck, and more shouts. Plant tried to make out what was being shouted. Was there a splash? Afterwards Plant could not be sure whether he'd heard one or not. What he mainly heard was Felix and Ghostly carrying on their reminiscences of the days of print undistracted. And then Claire came clattering down the stairway.

'Help!' she yelled at them, 'quick, help, Murray's gone overboard.'

She went back up to the deck. Plant followed. Felix and Ghostly peered up after him.

'He went over here,' Claire, said, standing at one side of the deck, rather pointlessly as the boat was still surging ahead.

'Tell whoever's at the wheel to stop,' Plant said.

'Sasha's gone to tell him,' she said.

But the *Jolly Britannia* was still ploughing on. It took what seemed an age before stopping. By the time that Sasha had been understood and what had happened had been registered, they were way past where Murray had gone overboard. The power was cut back and the boat slowed, rocking from side to side, and then gradually turned in a wide circle before heading back slowly, cautiously, in the direction it had come. And then the motor was cut in order to hear Murray, if he was calling out.

But there was nothing to hear, nothing to see. Just the dark water of the harbour. No beams of moonlight, no inverted reflections of the city, no flashing buoys, no splashing, no cries for help, no sign of movement, no sign of anything, nothing but darkness and the dulled, indistinct droning of marine engines that could be kilometres away.

'He just went over the side,' Claire said. 'Sasha was standing there and she took Liz's typescript out of her backpack and Murray reached out and took hold of it with one hand and he was making a call on his phone with the other and then it was like he slipped or lost his balance or something and his hands were full and he couldn't hold onto the rail and he went over the side and...'

She tailed off.

Sasha told the same story.

'Was there a struggle?' Plant asked.

'No, why would there be?' Sasha said. 'He just reached out for the typescript and took it while I was zipping up my backpack.'

'So you didn't try to stop him?'

'No, why would I? I was busy with the backpack anyway.'

'So he just took the pages and what – fell? slipped? jumped?'

'Sort of slipped and fell,' Sasha said.

Plant turned to Claire.

'I suppose so.'

'You suppose.'

'Well, why would he have jumped?'

'Was there an argument?' Plant asked.

'There was nothing to argue about,' Sasha said. 'Murray and Claire had agreed it wasn't worth publishing. It was all old stuff. Nothing new. Not enough to make a book. So why would they argue?'

The water police were called and they arrived, sirens howling. The surface of the water was scanned with powerful searchlights, but nothing showed up. Not Murray, anyway. Nor the unpublished pages of *What I Did and How, When and Why I Did It*. Had he taken them with him and never let go? Would they have slipped from his hand and sunk to the bottom of the harbour, weighted down by metal bulldog clips holding them together? Or had they fallen apart, separate pages scattered by the current, to wash up once in a while on beaches and in rock pools? There was no sign of them floating on the surface of the waters. No more than there was any sign of Murray.

There were statements. Interviews. Felix and Ghostly gave their best, analysis, speculation, context.

'But you didn't actually see him go over?'

'He'd been saying...'

'Were you out on the deck when he fell?'

'Did he fall or was he..?'

They could have gone on for hours. They did, summoning up phrases, interpretations, possibilities, talking to each other about it, so what if the police didn't want to hear their analyses, their inside information, their background data. In the heyday of print they could each have phoned in their exclusive account in time for the late edition of the morning papers. But the papers had already gone to bed.

Ghostly gazed at the waters reflectively, silently summoning up an eyewitness account for his blog: 'Over the side with hardly a splash, I was there when it happened. I heard the last ever heard or seen of Murray Brittan, not even a farewell message from the media magnate whose words once circled the world. The night was pitch black. The dark of the moon. We scoured the leaden surface of the harbour for any sight of him. Distantly on the shore lights flickered and went off in bedroom after bedroom. But there were no lights where Murray vanished, neither stars nor moon nor man-made. It was as if sound and picture had gone at the touch of a remote.'

Plant happily declared his absence from the scene.

'I was down in the saloon talking to Felix and Ghostly. Well, listening to them...'

'And when he went overboard?'

'We were down below, the three of us. I mean, we didn't know anyone had gone overboard until people started shouting.'

'And then?'

'Then Claire came down and told us and I went up on deck.'

'And what did you see?'

'Nothing. Well, Claire was leaning over the side. Sasha had gone up to the wheel. We were still surging ahead.'

'Surging?'

'Whatever. Going. I don't know how fast. We hadn't slowed down, I know that.'

'And then?'

'And then we stopped and swung round and headed back.'

'Did you see any sign of Mr Brittan?'

'No. Nothing.'

'Did anyone dive overboard to attempt to find him?'

'No. I doubt if any of them would be up to it.'

'And you?'

'Me? I'm not a swimmer.'

'Is that so?'

'I can float. Breast stroke. Dog paddle. But that's about it.'

'And no one else jumped in.'

'No.'

'Why not?'

'You'd have to ask them. I imagine they didn't see any point. No one seemed to know where he'd gone in exactly.'

There was no response. Was it scepticism? Perfunctoriness? Common sense?

And why hadn't Sasha jumped? All fitness gear and athleticism. Maybe she'd assumed there was no need. Could Murray swim? Maybe she knew he could and expected to see him surface. Or thought he could. Maybe she couldn't.

The police remained stony faced. Impassive.

Chapter Thirty

'Well, they would, wouldn't they?' Fullalove said. 'They're not stupid. They've been through situations like this scores of times before. They know when things don't add up, when they don't smell right.'

'They still haven't found the body.'

'Probably never will. Unless they can get hold of one roughly the right size and shape and age. And they'll probably have to mash up its face to make it unrecognizable. Say it got caught in the screws of a cruise ship. But then you've got problems with DNA. So probably not.'

'You reckon?'

'You don't imagine he's dead, do you?'

Plant had wondered. Maybe Sasha or Claire had belted Murray on the head and given him a shove overboard. Maybe the pair of them were in it together, between them they could have overpowered him and pushed him over the side. It wasn't impossible. He suggested it to Fullalove.

'In which case the body would have turned up by now.'

'Really?'

'Should have. Unless it was weighed down by guns strapped to his arm-pit and ankle, or a money belt of gold bars wrapped round his waist, or built-up steel-capped boots. Except that you tell me he was bare-footed and wearing shorts and T-shirt, so rather than being weighed down, I'd suggest he was dressed for swimming with the minimum of impediment from clothing. And with that colour-coordinated outfit, more specifically for swimming in the dark. And no one has suggested suicide, that's never an option with types like him. But if he had been planning suicide, he would have been wearing a suit and waistcoat with lead weights in every pocket. No, forget it. This is just another version of the old classic "fall off the back of the boat" story. Or whatever. Go for a swim and don't come back. Harold Holt. John Stonehouse. Robert Maxwell. It's a tired old copy of a done-to-death story. A real cheap one. Way out of copyright. Typical of media types, always too cheap to come up with an original, always go for a re-run.'

'They found Stonehouse.'

'Of course. That's the point I'm making. He didn't die. The old vanishing trick. And don't say they found Maxwell's body. They issued a photograph of a shrouded figure with a gross bulging belly and face covered. And people believed it. Brilliant.'

'So you reckon Murray's...?'

'Alive and well and living in the Middle East or South America or South East Asia, with a harem of local beauties and a swag of money safely stashed away in Switzerland or somewhere. I imagine so, don't you?'

'How would he have managed it?'

'Easy enough to do,' Fullalove said. 'From the time the *Jolly Britannia* sets off he's arranged for it to be shadowed. Special services type inflatable, black as a media magnate's soul, ultra-quiet motor but a great turn of speed when it's needed. It's hanging back astern, waiting, and when there are no other craft around and he's ready to jump he just sends a message on his phone and then over he goes, he hasn't eaten anything, he hasn't drunk alcohol, he's not going to get a cramp or anything, he doesn't splash around, he just floats and the *Jolly Britannia* keeps on going, and he's left way back there, T-shirt and shorts, bare feet, easy to swim, no heavy clothes dragging him down, so as long as he keeps his mouth shut and doesn't show his teeth he just merges into the black night, the inflatable picks him up, they're all in black, he's all in black, everything pretty well invisible.'

'And then?'

'I guess they take him ashore somewhere, he dries himself off, puts on a business suit and goes to the airport, ticket already booked, false passport, new identity, out of the country, new life.'

'It would take a lot of planning,' Plant objected.

'If you're planning on faking your own death and taking on a new identity, then you would be up for a lot of planning, don't you reckon? He could have set it all up years ago when it was easier to get false ID. Long-term contingency plan for someone like him.'

'I suppose so,' Plant agreed.

'Don't be depressed about it,' Fullalove said. 'You played your part perfectly.'

'What part?'

'The bumbling private investigator. The Inspector Plod of private eyes. It used to be the police were the stupid ones and the private eyes the smart ones, but here you are, reversing the archetype, brilliant.'

'I don't feel I achieved anything,' Plant said.

'Exactly. You weren't meant to.'

'I didn't even find the manuscript.'

'Don't worry about it. No one wanted a manuscript to turn up, they wanted to bury any trace of it. Or drown it, as it happened. Murray was finished. The sexual harassment stuff was the last straw. He wasn't going to be able to keep the lid on that any longer, whether Lambastier's stuff got made public or not. It was just a matter of time before more women he'd monstered came forward and it wouldn't have been forgotten words from the grave, it would have been full-on, first-person singular, personal accounts, stories in the press, social media posts, television interviews. Trial by media. He couldn't deal with that and with his collapsing business. Can't fight on two fronts. Best thing was to cut and run.

'You'll find he was in deep shit. His business was down the tubes. He would probably have been trading while bankrupt, effectively, so he was looking at being banned from company directorships. Which was going to be a lot more serious than the sex charges. This was about money and fraud, forget all the bad behaviour blather. So he would have transferred whatever assets he could lay his hands on out of the country and planned his disappearance. If there'd been an employee's pension fund he could have got his hands on, he'd have ripped that off too. Maybe there was.

'He'd have been planning it for ages. It wasn't just the fear of being exposed as a sexual predator. He'd always been like that. I doubt he ever thought there was any problem about it. But what he couldn't deal with was the way his business was going down. He'd had to close his magazine when the advertising migrated online. He wasn't savvy enough to get into the internet. His book publishing division was losing it, no one was buying books anymore, not the sort he'd been publishing. He'd been heavily into property development and that was all going bad with oversupply. And he would've realized, being a chiseller himself, that even if he bought the copy off Sasha and kept it suppressed or destroyed it, another copy was going to pop up. Arranging to get hold of it from Sasha when he did was a bonus, stop the story from breaking for a bit longer. But given the mood of the times, the sexual harassment stories were going to break anyway, manuscript or no manuscript. All he wanted to do was to get out before a whole swag of stuff surfaced, sexual, financial, whatever. And once he'd disappeared and been born again with a new identity, what did it matter?

'And you were his star witness. One of them, anyway. With a private investigator and a couple of old, would-be, investigative journalists on board, how can anybody say that he didn't drown?'

'Maybe he did.'

'Not your problem, anyway.'

Plant reflected. Quite right, it wasn't. None of it was. Maybe he didn't have any problems at all. His spirits lifted.

'Here, roll yourself a smoke, why don't you?'

'Good idea,' Plant agreed, spirits lifting some more.

'Of course, there's no way of telling if the manuscript Sasha handed over to Murray was real or not.'

'What do you mean?'

'How do you know there really were these bits cut out of Lambastier's first book? How do you know Sasha and her aunt didn't fake it?'

'I guess I don't.'

'And you don't know if Sasha was working for Murray, or for herself, or for someone else.'

'No.'

'Same thing with your employer.'

'True.'

'Exactly. So what do you know?'

'I was hired to find a manuscript, not to find out who wanted it and who they might have been working for.'

'But you didn't.'

'Well, it did turn up, even if it got lost.'

'Maybe. Anyway, who cares any more?' Fullalove asked, in rhetorical mode. 'No one. We've moved way beyond innocent surprise at CIA recruitment of literary celebrities or at media moguls' criminality and sexual predatoriness. It's everyday news now, banks laundering dirty money, society coke dealers, the days when we were surprised, let alone shocked, are long past. Even the sexual harassment stuff is old news now. We've heard it all before. So what?

'Tragic, isn't it? All this fuss and search and stuff about this missing manuscript and it's not even a manuscript, not even something she was writing, just the off-cuts from when she was writing her first book, if it was even that. Before she made it. When she had a talent.'

Chapter Thirty-one

Plant presented himself at Claire's apartment. Or whoever's apartment it was.

'I had to make sure that there wasn't anything anywhere out there,' she said. 'I want to be able to say definitely that there is no manuscript. We searched for it thoroughly and there is no evidence that it exists.'

'Survives,' Plant said.

'What do you mean?'

'Well, it may have existed and been found and destroyed. So we can say it no longer survives. Otherwise you're implying there never was a manuscript.'

'Precisely. I want to put an end to that rumour altogether. Otherwise people will never stop asking about it unless we make it clear there never was a manuscript.'

'What about the stories?' he asked. 'Are you sure Sasha or Hilly haven't made a copy?'

'No.'

'No what?'

'I'm not sure they didn't make a copy. But it doesn't matter. They can't publish anything. I'm Liz's literary executor. I hold the copyrights.'

'They could sell it to a collector.'

'Who'd want to collect it?'

'You don't think there are collectors out there collecting her work?'

'I doubt it. Their best bet would be to sell it to the State Library. They might be able to raise a bit of cash for it that way. Add it to Liz's papers.'

'Some biographer will turn it up.'

'What biographer? No one's shown any interest so far. By the time anyone's ploughed through her papers everyone will be dead anyway, no one will care.'

'Not even Murray,' Plant said. 'Maybe it'll pop up one day. She'll be forgotten and then rediscovered, revived, written about, her books reissued, remaindered, removed from library shelves since no one's borrowed them, consigned to deposit, and more oblivion.'

Claire ignored him.

'But if Sasha or Hilly did make a copy and you have the rights, then you could reissue the stories with the suppressed ones restored. It would be a way of getting the rest of her books back into print.'

'Liz still has her reputation,' she said. 'She was a prize bitch but I don't see the need to make her look worse.'

'It would get her name around again.'

'No doubt. And no doubt she'd have thought it was a great idea. But no. This time she misses out, tough luck, sis.'

So he wasn't going to be asked to try to extract a copy from Sasha or Hilly that they just might have. Which was something of a relief. He did a quick search for the phrase he needed. Lead us not into temptation. That was it. And while at it, he silently summoned up the rest of the prayer. Deliver us from evil.

'I guess that's it then,' Plant said. 'No missing manuscript. End of story. Though usually a body overboard would mean the beginning of the story.'

Claire said nothing, just looked at him, blankly, not even interrogatively.

'I still find it hard to believe,' she said.

'Believe what?'

'That there wasn't a last book.'

'On anything in particular?'

'Herself, of course. How could she not have written an autobiography? She was such a narcissist.'

'Maybe there were things that couldn't be told.'

‘Then she’d just have lied.’

She shook her head slowly.

Another dissatisfied client.

Where was the job satisfaction?

Books by Michael Wilding from Arcadia and Australian Scholarly

THE PRISONER OF MOUNT WARNING

ISBN 978-1-921509-56-8

'With a detective called Plant and a journey from Sydney to the dope fields of Byron Bay, the private eye novel has come a long way from Raymond Chandler ... the detective novel's move into an era of magic mushrooms and free love.' – *Sydney Morning Herald.*

'This satirical odyssey from an Australian literary legend has his protagonist heading north to find himself, among other things. Charles Dorritt recovers from a breakdown by doing a writing course and decides to write of his torture and slavery at the hands of the security services. He's pursued by Plant, who's been hired to dissuade him from revealing all... Wilding was at the forefront of a rebellious Australian literary movement in the '70s; in this book, he weaves a narrative of personal, literary and political dimensions into an entertaining yarn.' – Phil Brown, *Brisbane News.*

THE MAGIC OF IT

ISBN 978-1-921875-37-3

'The truth in this fiction is at least as entertaining as what has been invented. This a clever, offbeat rendering of a crime story with a smattering of illustrations by the great Australian artist Garry Shead and a protagonist who surely will be back.' – Emma Young, *Sydney Morning Herald.*

'With his previous Plant novel, *The Prisoner of Mount Warning*, Michael Wilding broke new ground. Plant investigates, not the petty individual crimes like kidnapping, murder or extortion, but the big picture – the intellectual and political follies of the age. True to the genre, Plant's cases start small and grow but, unlike the books in which the bodies pile up, with Wilding the unstable underpinning of modern industrialised society is laid bare. And made hilariously funny.' – Peter Corris.

ASIAN DAWN

ISBN 978-1-921875-39-7

'A compelling narrative with a cast of enigmatic figures. The exotic bar singer, the speech writer for hire, the publisher with guerrilla connections, the sex-addicted expatriate and the missing political scientist are only some of the fascinating cast of characters ... Wilding blends his wit with the comic and the bizarre in a novel that surprises by its twists and turns. This is a novel that enhances our understanding of the Australian-Asian relationship while at the same time providing an exciting, fast-moving thriller.' – Irina Dunn, *Network News.*

'*Asian Dawn* is a fast-paced read with lots of seedy sex and compromising secrets, plus a few well aimed jabs at the academic world.' – Cameron Woodhead, *Sydney Morning Herald.*

IN THE VALLEY OF THE WEED

ISBN 978-1-925333-97-8

'The Plant novels, of which this is the fifth ... are hybrids of satire and crime fiction, too funny to be called bleak, but concealing a complex seriousness of purpose. At the instigation of his old friend Fullalove, Plant in his capacity as private detective goes looking for an academic who has been suspended for thoughtcrime and has subsequently disappeared. The least attractive aspects of neoliberalism and its consequences come in for some savage critique in this intermittently hilarious novel.' – Kerryn Goldsworthy, *The Age.*

LITTLE DEMON

ISBN 978-1-925588-73-6

'Wilding writes the Plant novels with apparent ease. At the same time, he dares those among us who are averse to conspiracy theories to wonder whether we have been too sceptical.' – Peter Pierce, *Weekend Australian.*

'Plant's case may have started out as a simple criminal investigation, but it swiftly, and unforgettably, shines bright lights onto the way we live, and some of the reasons why.' – Derek Turner, *Spectator Australia.*

SUPERFLUOUS MEN

ISBN 978-1-921509-47-6

'You have a way of being gloomily funny that speaks for all the early-retired and those who cannot avoid weary contempt for the bureaucrats both in and out of the universities.' – Frank Kermode

'Wilding is a wicked observer of human foibles and bureaucracy; and he has an evilly good ear for the dopey chit-chat that so often passes for high flown discourse and earnest-speak. It's very funny.' – Diana Simmonds, *SAM*

'Why should the reader be interested in Michael's protagonists, these "drunken old men of a certain age, forgotten by the world and reciprocating its disregard"? Mostly it's because they are extremely funny, their verbal witticisms serving to starkly and sometimes surprisingly emphasise their point. Wilding's satirical edge evokes in the reader not only sly smiles of recognition but outright guffaws of full-blown belly laughter.' – Irina Dunn, *Quadrant*

WILD BLEAK BOHEMIA: MARCUS CLARKE, ADAM LINDSAY GORDON AND HENRY KENDALL: A DOCUMENTARY

ISBN 978-1-925003-80-2

Winner of the Prime Minister's Literary Award for non fiction and the Colin Roderick Award.

'A superb study of colonial culture ... Wilding's splendid book,' – Peter Pierce, *Weekend Australian.*

'This wonderful book ... this outstanding, original documentary,' – Patrick Morgan, *Quadrant.*

'A remarkable exercise in literary history ... an extraordinarily rich picture,' – Paul de Serville, *Newtown Review of Books.*

GROWING WILD

ISBN 978-1-925333-10-7

'An important historical record of a seminal period in Australian writing, as well as a revealing insight into the life and mind of a writer... It is both an entertaining and visionary book on how to sustain a literary life and at the same time remain true to key intellectual values and beliefs.' – Ross Fitzgerald, *Weekend Australian.*

'This entertaining, instructive memoir by veteran Australian writer and publisher Michael Wilding ... a memoir of one particular life and also of the milieus and movements it intersected with and animated: those of scholars, academics, poets, fiction writers, anarchists and activists, in various permutations. *Growing Wild* is the memory of someone who always took notice, and always took notes.' – Inez Baranay, *Newtown Review of Books.*

Printed in Australia
AUOW01n1225170818
301596AU00001B/1

9 781925 801378